Praise for the Tj Jensen Mystery Series

"Daley's characters come to life on the page. Her novels are filled with a little mystery and a little romance which makes for a murderous adventure."

— Tonya Kappes,
USA Today Bestselling Author of *Fixin' To Die*

"Daley's mysteries offer as much sizzle and pop as fireworks on a hot summer's day."

— Mary Kennedy,
Author of The Dream Club Mysteries

"I'm a huge fan of Kathi's books. I think I've read every one. Without a doubt, she's a gifted cozy mystery author and I eagerly await each new release!"

— Dianne Harman,
Author of the High Desert Cozy Mysteries

"Intriguing, likeable characters, keep-you-guessing mysteries, and settings that literally transport you to Paradise...Daley's stories draw you in and keep you glued until the very last page."

— Tracy Weber,
Agatha-Nominated Author of the Downward Dog Mysteries

"Daley really knows how to write a top-notch cozy."

— *MJB Reviewers*

"Kathi Daley writes a story with a puzzling cold-case mystery while highlighting...the love of home, family, and good friends."

— *Chatting About Cozies*

Pumpkins
IN
PARADISE

The Tj Jensen Mystery Series
by Kathi Daley

Pumpkins

A
TJ JENSEN
MYSTERY

IN

PARADISE

KATHI DALEY

HENERY PRESS

PUMPKINS IN PARADISE
A Tj Jensen Mystery
Part of the Henery Press Mystery Collection

Second Edition | September 2016

Henery Press, LLC
www.henerypress.com

Trade Paperback ISBN-13: 978-1-63511-089-0
Digital epub ISBN-13: 978-1-63511-090-6
Kindle ISBN-13: 978-1-63511-091-3
Hardcover Paperback ISBN-13: 978-1-63511-092-0

Printed in the United States of America

This book is dedicated to my friend and mentor Paul Dinas,
without whose guidance, patience, and inspiration,
the book would not have been written.

ACKNOWLEDGMENTS

They say it takes a village and I have a great one.

I want to thank all my friends who hang out over at my Kathi Daley Books Group page on Facebook. This exceptional group help me not only with promotion but with helpful suggestion and feedback as well.

I want to thank the bloggers who have pretty much adopted me and have helped me to build a fantastic social media presence. There are too many to list, but I want to specifically recognize Lisa Kelley for taking in a brand new author and introducing me around.

I want to thank my fellow authors who I run to all the time when I don't know how to do something or how to deal with a situation. I have to say that the cozy mystery family is about as close-knit a family as you are likely to find anywhere.

I want to thank Bruce Curran for generously helping me with all my techy questions and Ricky Turner for help with my webpage.

I want to thank my graphic designer Jessica Fisher for all my flashy ads and headers.

I want to thank Randy Ladenheim-Gil for making what I write legible.

I want to thank Art Molinares for welcoming me so enthusiastically to the Henery Press family and a special thank you to Erin George and the entire editing crew who have been so incredibly awesome and fun to work with.

And last but certainly not least, I want to thank my super-husband Ken for allowing me time to write by taking care of everything else (and I mean everything).

CHAPTER 1

Friday, October 22

Tj Jensen carefully parallel parked her 4Runner on Lake Front Road in front of Tiz the Season, the retail store where she'd brought her half-sisters, Ashley and Gracie, to buy their Halloween costumes. The entire downtown section of the lakefront community of Serenity, Nevada was decorated for the upcoming Halloween festivities. Bright yellow aspen trees lining the sidewalks were draped with orange and white twinkle lights, while hundreds of scarecrows and huge orange pumpkins were displayed in front of brightly lit shops inviting the casual passerby in from the crisp fall air.

"Oh, look," Gracie gasped as she climbed out of the vehicle and noticed the huge fall village, complete with an operating train, in the front window. Ashley and Gracie trotted over to watch as the small train chugged, tooted, and smoked its way through the miniature town square. The store's owner added to the village each season. This year a delightful traveling carnival with a revolving Ferris wheel and a brightly painted merry-go-round were prominently displayed alongside the charming Main Street.

"Okay, we're in, we're out," Tj warned as she locked the car door and slung her purse over her shoulder. "You need to be at dance in half an hour."

"There is no dance," Gracie informed her.

Tj turned to look directly at the brown-haired, brown-eyed kindergartener while Ashley walked around the edge of the building to get a closer look at the miniature village. "It's Friday. You always have dance on Friday."

"Miss Marsha sent a note. I gave it to you on Monday." Gracie's ringlets bounced as she shuffled impatiently.

Tj did remember something about a note.

"She had to go to the dynocologist to get a baby," Gracie informed her.

Marsha and her husband of four years had been trying to conceive for a while, but Tj was surprised she'd told her students as much. "She told you she was going to the gynecologist?"

"No. She said she had a pointment, but Bethany said she was getting a baby from a dynocologist 'cause she needed to get fertilizer for her eggs." Bethany Sherwood was a precocious five-year-old who, in Tj's opinion, was a bit too informed for her age. "Dance is going to be on lasterday."

"Lasterday isn't a word," corrected red-haired, green-eyed Ashley as she returned from the window. "Dance class has been rescheduled to tomorrow. Can we go in now?" she asked impatiently. "The place is packed. All the good stuff will be gone."

"There's plenty of good stuff." Tj grabbed each of her sisters' hands and opened the front door to deafening noise as excited children ran up and down crowded aisles in search of the perfect costume. Picking up a bright orange hand basket, she pushed her way into the throng.

"Mom said that last year when I wanted to be Hannah

Montana, and I had to be Strawberry Shortcake. Do you know how many seven-year-olds went trick-or-treating as Strawberry Shortcake? One," Ashley continued without waiting for Tj to answer. "My social life was totally ruined."

"What social life?" Tj teased. "You were seven."

Ashley sighed loudly and rolled her eyes, but Tj noticed a teary glaze to which her independent sister would never admit. While Gracie would curl up in her lap and cry herself to sleep if she was feeling sad, Ashley hid her feelings behind a mask of mature indifference that Tj had rarely been able to crack. Tj paused and reconsidered her hurried approach to the errand. Despite her best intentions, she'd made many mistakes with Ashley in the three months since her mother died and the courts had appointed her legal guardian of two half-sisters she barely knew.

"You're right," Tj apologized, blue eyes locking with pale green ones. "I'm sorry I didn't have the chance to bring you earlier in the month. I'm sure there will be plenty of good stuff, but if there's not, we'll try another store."

"Okay," Ashley conceded, turning to wipe away a tear before anyone noticed.

"How about witches?" Tj suggested as she tried to lighten the mood by holding a mask with a huge wart on the nose in front of her face.

Ashley placed a crown from a nearby table on her head. "I want to be a princess."

"I want to be Belle," Gracie insisted.

"Belle's too provincial," replied Ashley. "I want to be Jasmine."

Provincial? Tj watched as her intellectually advanced but socially awkward sister skipped down the aisle toward a table overflowing with dresses and accessories of all colors and sizes.

Hurrying to catch up, she pulled a blue dress from the pile. "This looks like your size."

"That's Sleeping Beauty," Ashley complained. "I really want to be Jasmine."

"Okay." Tj set her purse on the floor and dug through the disorganized pile of costumes throngs of shoppers had tried on and discarded. At one point, Tj figured, the delicate outfits, which the sign on the wall promised came with dress, crown, and plastic shoes, had been neatly packaged and organized by princess and size. Today, however, the clothes were piled onto a table in total disarray. "How about this?" She held up a dress and a pair of shoes in front of Gracie.

"Shoes are right, but that's Cinderella's dress," Gracie whined. "I want to be Belle."

Wasn't one princess the same as any other? Fancy dress, high-heeled slippers, and sparkly crown? Tj set down the pair of shoes on the floor next to her purse, texted an SOS to her best friend, Jenna Elston, and waited for a reply. Tj attributed her lack of knowledge of anything princess to the fact that her mother had deserted her when she was only three years old, subjecting her to an upbringing in an all-male household. Tj conveniently blamed her mom's desertion for most, if not all, of her feminine deficiencies.

But, if she was honest with herself, they were probably more genetic than environmental. Most days Tj wore her tomboyishness as a badge of honor. She could outhike, outski, and outrun most of the men in town of a comparable age. But today, waist deep in princess dresses, she really could use Jenna's help.

Tj's phone beeped when Jenna texted back: yellow dress, dark hair, B & B.

"B and B?" Tj said out loud.

"*Beauty and the Beast*," Gracie informed her as she tossed a bag of Snickers into their basket.

Tj didn't know how she would have managed when her mother and her third husband died in a car accident three months earlier if it weren't for Jenna and her unwavering support. It helped that Jenna had two young daughters about the same age as her sisters. Unfortunately, Tj'd had to call on Jenna during the past few months more often than she cared to confess.

"Excuse me." Tj turned and grabbed the upper arm of the high school-aged clerk. "I'm looking for a Belle costume."

"There's more Disney stuff at the end of aisle twelve."

"Thanks." Tj grabbed Gracie's hand and turned to change direction.

"Do you have Jasmine costumes?" Ashley asked before the clerk could walk away.

"I think we're out of Jasmine, but we have a few Snow Whites left."

"Snow White is for babies. I want to be Jasmine," Ashley insisted.

"Sorry. You should have come in earlier. Just a week until Halloween, you know."

Ashley put her hands on her hips and shot Tj a glance that said *I told you so*.

"Besides," he added, "you really should be Ariel. Ariel has beautiful red hair like you. I think I might have a costume that will fit you in the back."

"Really?" Ashley beamed.

"Yeah, I'll check. Just wait right here."

"He said I was beautiful," Ashley gushed as the clerk went in search of the costume. "He said I looked *just* like Ariel."

"You do honey, you do."

"What about Belle?" Gracie started to dance around in that special I-gotta-go way.

"As soon as the clerk gets back with Ashley's costume."

Tj watched as a woman with a crying infant strapped to her chest, a toddler in her arms, and a preschooler on each side schlepped an armload of princess separates up to the mile-long line at the checkout stand. Tj loved Halloween, but sometimes she wondered what had happened to homemade costumes like the ones she'd worn as a child. Toss a sheet over your head, cut out a couple of eyeholes, and you were good to go. No wading through piles of dresses or spending a month's mad money on an outfit the girls would wear only once.

"Here we go." The clerk had returned from the storage room. "An Ariel costume for my redheaded princess and a Belle costume for my dark-haired princess." Both girls screamed in delight as the clerk handed them complete unopened sets of the princesses of their choice. Dress, shoes, crown, all matching, in exactly the right size.

"Anything else?" he asked.

"Thanks, but I'll just take the princess costumes for now." Tj grabbed Gracie's hand and headed toward the long line that awaited her at the checkout stand.

CHAPTER 2

Fifty minutes later, Tj sat behind the registration desk of Maggie's Hideaway, waiting for the last of the weekend arrivals to check in. Echo, her hundred-and-thirty-pound mountain dog, was lying on the rug next to her, sound asleep except for the occasional whimper as he actively participated in what must be a rollicking doggy dream. After the mayhem of the day, the world once again seemed balanced and serene.

Huge picture windows lined the back wall, transporting the beauty of the lake and surrounding forest into the interior of the mountain lodge. It was a perfect fall day, cool but sunny, with just a few clouds hinting at the storm she knew was brewing over the summit. A lone coyote walked along the now-deserted beach as squirrels scurried across the wooden deck gathering pine nuts for the long winter ahead. Pouring herself a cup of coffee from the sideboard, Tj selected several ginger snaps from the tray, then wandered over to the desk to check the reservation sheet. There were three guests who hadn't checked in yet. She hoped they'd all arrive in a timely fashion, since Jenna and her daughters, Kristi and Kari, were coming for dinner and movie night. Jenna's husband Dennis, a firefighter for the Serenity Fire Department, was on duty for an overnight shift.

"Seen your dad?" Grandpa Ben walked up behind her. A

mountain of a man, well over six feet with broad shoulders and a deep baritone voice. He filled the room with his presence. Dressed in dirt-stained work jeans and sturdy boots, Ben looked much younger than his sixty-eight years in spite of his head of thick white hair.

"I think he was moving boats. Why?"

"Headin' over to The Grill to help decorate for the Halloween Party next week, but we can't seem to find that box of decorations we used last year."

"Did you check the attic space above the garage?" Tj asked. "I think I saw some stuff up there. I've been meaning to get it down and decorate the house. The staff did a good job with the rest of the resort."

"Yeah, it looks real nice." The decorating crew had gone all out this year, with a pumpkin patch on the front lawn, an old-fashioned horse-drawn wagon filled with bales of hay near the resort's entrance, and brightly dressed scarecrows scattered throughout. The lobby featured garlands of brightly colored fall leaves, wreaths, and festive bouquets of seasonal flowers. "Guess I'll head over to the house and see if I can find the decorations. I'll put the stuff for the house in the mud room."

"Thanks, Grandpa."

"By the way," Ben added, "Bookman wanted me to tell you he can't make dinner this week since his agent will be in town and next Monday doesn't look good either. Guess there's a town council meeting that night. Wanted to know if we could do it another night."

Ben's friend Bookman, a.k.a. bestselling author R. L. Hellerman, was one of the five elected citizens who sat on Serenity's town council. "I thought the council meeting wasn't for another three weeks."

"It's not. At least the normal monthly town meeting isn't.

There's a special session on November first to discuss the permit Lloyd Benson applied for. I guess there's some urgency for reasons of which I'm not privy, and Lloyd didn't want to wait until the regular town meeting."

"What's he tearing down now?" Tj sighed.

"He's not tearing anything down this time," Ben informed her. "He reapplied for a permit for those condos down by the lake he's been trying to build for the past couple of years."

Tj frowned. "How is he going to do that? I thought the whole thing was a no-go if he didn't have Zachary's land as an access point."

Ben shrugged. "I really don't know. Maybe Zachary finally sold."

"He wouldn't do that," Tj insisted. "He was adamant about not wanting people traipsing through his property. There must be more to the story."

Ben shrugged. "Guess you can ask Zachary about it."

Tj frowned. "Yeah, I'll stop by tomorrow." Zachary Collins was an eighty-six-year-old recluse who valued his privacy and would never sell access to his land. Would he? Surely he hadn't sold out to Lloyd after all these years.

"Guess I'll head on over to the house. What do you want me to do with the pile of pumpkins on the dining-room table?"

Tj groaned. In a moment of temporary insanity, she'd volunteered to carve twenty-five pumpkins for the annual pumpkin festival. "Sorry. I totally forgot those were being delivered today."

"I'll move them into the mud room for now," Ben volunteered.

"Thanks, Grandpa."

*   *   *

After Ben left, Tj greeted a pair of identical-looking sexagenarians, each carrying two bags of identical size and color. "Welcome to Maggie's Hideaway. Are you checking in?" During the summer the lobby of Maggie's Hideaway was crowded with guests checking in and out every day of the week. But during the slower shoulder seasons, roughly the three months between summer and ski season, and then again between the end of ski season and the beginning of summer, most arrivals and departures were limited to a few weekend visitors.

"Maude and Millie Morrison," the twin on the right answered.

"We won an all-expense-paid trip," the twin on the left added.

"That's great. Radio contest?" Tj smiled at the pair, each of whom looked a lot like Aunt Bea from *The Andy Griffith Show*. Tj hadn't even been born when the show first aired, but her Grandma Maggie used to watch the reruns on cable before she passed away.

"No," Maude answered. "We received a letter in the mail informing us we'd been chosen to receive a ten-day trip. We don't remember entering a contest, but at our age we usually can't remember what we had for breakfast."

"This isn't a time-share, is it?" Millie asked.

"No, I can assure you the trip wasn't sponsored by Maggie's Hideaway." Tj glanced at the computer screen. "The reservation simply states the cabin was prepaid in full. Perhaps the trip was sponsored by one of the casinos? They sometimes offer special incentives to seniors."

"We're not here to gamble," Maude assured her.

"We're here to meet men," Millie added.

"Well, I'll be sure to keep my eyes open for good catches." Tj smiled. "I see you're staying in cabin twelve. It's one of our nicer two-bedrooms. Right on the beach, in an isolated cove surrounded by old growth pines with its own deck and hot tub. Very private for entertaining." Tj waved over a dark-haired teenager who had wandered in while she was speaking to the women. "This is Emily," she introduced her to the sisters. "She'll show you to your cabin and answer any questions you have along the way."

"Oh, aren't you adorable," Maude gushed. Emily possessed a petite doll-like figure, huge blue eyes framed with thick dark lashes, and fistfuls of thick curly hair.

"Love your shoes," Emily complimented the two women on their shiny white Sketchers as she reached down to pick up one of their bags, causing a book to fall from the top in the process. *"Twenty-five Ways to Please a Man,"* Emily read aloud as she picked up the book.

"Sister and I figured we were a bit late out of the starting gate so could use some advice," Maude explained.

"Just read the first five," Millie joined in. "Figured you really only need the first two, but we brought the book along just in case."

Tj and Emily looked at each other, trying not to laugh.

"Still that thing with the whipped cream sounded fun," Maude reminded her sister. "Maybe we should have brought some."

"If you decide you need it just let me know and I'll have some brought to your cabin," Tj promised.

Tj watched the group walk away. She certainly didn't want to be Maude and Millie's age and still looking for a man. After her mom died and her sisters came to live with her, she and her ex-boyfriend Tyler had parted ways. Tj knew he wasn't looking for anything serious, but it hurt that he'd tossed her aside like yesterday's laundry once it had become apparent that carefree and unencumbered were things of the past.

Tj looked around the room for Echo. He had vacated his napping spot behind the registration desk and wandered over to the seating area near the fireplace, where a man who appeared to be in his early thirties, with wavy blond hair, deep blue eyes, and a body an underwear model would envy, was reading an R. L. Hellerman mystery. Tj made it a policy never to get involved with guests, but she had to admit this one was tempting. She watched as the man stopped reading and set his book aside when Echo approached. Echo was friendly, but his size could be intimidating to guests who didn't know him.

Echo sat at the man's feet, placing one paw on his knee in greeting. Tj didn't think the man had stayed with them before, but Echo, who could be standoffish with people he didn't know, acted like the two of them were old friends. The man said something to the large dog and began scratching him behind the ears in exactly the way he loved best.

Tj walked across the room, picked up a log from the pile, and tossed it on the blaze burning warmly in the fireplace before approaching the man. "I apologize for my dog," she said in greeting. Echo's head was in the man's lap by this point. "Normally he doesn't bother the guests. I don't know what's gotten into him."

"It's not a problem," the man said with a smile. "I like dogs and generally they like me. I had to leave my lab at home, so I'm glad for the company."

"Well, now that you've scratched Echo in his favorite spot, he'll probably come over and bug you every time he sees you. If he becomes a pest, just let me know."

"It won't be a problem. I promise." The man continued to run his hands thorough Echo's coat.

Tj grinned. She knew she should call Echo to her side and walk away, but she found herself lingering.

"R. L. Hellerman fan?" She nodded toward the book he had been reading before Echo wandered over.

"I love his stuff. He really pulls you into the mystery right from the beginning. You a fan?"

"The biggest. He lives in Serenity, you know. In fact, he's a good friend of the family. I can introduce you, if you'd like."

The man's eyes lit up with anticipation. "Really? That would be great. I'll be here all week."

"I'll let you know the next time he's at the resort," Tj promised. "He usually pops in every day or two. My name's Tj, by the way."

"Kyle Donovan." The man held out his hand.

"Here on vacation?"

"Job interview. I got laid off six months ago, and I've been looking ever since."

"I've lived here all my life. Maybe I can put in a good word for you. In a town this size, I know pretty much everyone."

"The company I'm interviewing with is called the Repository."

Tj frowned. "Never heard of them. What kind of company is it?"

Kyle sat back as Echo wandered over to his favorite rug in front of the fireplace to wait. "I'm not sure. I work as a computer programmer, so I've worked for a variety of different types of enterprises. This company didn't go into detail about what they do exactly, but they sent me a letter offering me a job at an obscene rate of pay, so I decided to check it out."

Tj frowned. "Sounds…"

"Hinky? I know. Believe me, I changed my mind about coming a hundred times. The letter said the stay would be completely paid for, so I figured what did I have to lose? If the job's a fake, I still get a free vacation in this beautiful place."

"Yeah, but what if whoever sent the letter is a psycho? Or a serial killer?"

"Why would a serial killer pay for me to stay at a resort before offing me?"

"Good point."

"The woman who checked me in said the reservation was prepaid in full by a man named John Henry. I guess he works for the company I'm interviewing with."

"Probably." Tj noticed that a woman who looked to be in her mid-twenties was struggling to wrestle several bags onto a service cart. She hoped it was Carmen Lewis, her final guest of the day. "Well, good luck, and if you decide you could use a good word, let me know."

"Thanks. I will."

CHAPTER 3

Saturday, October 23

Tj first met the elusive Zachary Collins on Halloween night almost fourteen years earlier. The kids in town made up all kinds of rumors about the man who never left his estate. Most thought he was a vampire, others created a gruesome monster in their imagination, while a few thought he was nothing but a ghost. To this day Tj didn't know the entire story, but something had happened when Zachary was a young man. A car accident had left ugly scars on the right side of his once handsome face. Zachary was sensitive about the scars, but Tj suspected it was the emotional scars rather than the physical that had left him a lonely, bitter, recluse of a man.

On the Halloween night in question, Tj and her friends were out egging houses when they got bored and decided to check out the infamous haunted house. Since Tj, who was twelve at the time, was the only one small enough to slip through the narrow opening where the tall wrought-iron gate met the ten-foot wall, her friends dared her to sneak inside, knock on the door, then run away. Never one to turn down a dare, she had, Zachary had caught her, and in spite of the teasing she received from her friends, and her dad's concern over the friendship between a twelve-year-old girl and a seventy-two-year-old man, they'd been close ever since.

"Zachary," Tj called as she entered the dark, windowless room through the cellar door. "It's Tj. Are you down here?"

Zachary often preferred the complete lack of sunlight in the cellar, which he used as a sort of workroom. It wasn't a bad room, as cellars went. A worn rug covered the stone floor, and old but once expensive furniture was arranged comfortably around a long workbench he used to build his various inventions. The only truly personal touch was a photo of a handsome young man standing proudly next to a new Model T. Tj knew the man in the photo was Zachary's father who had bought the car, the first of its kind, hot off the assembly line in 1908.

"Zachary?" Tj stopped and looked around. The old wood stove, which usually heated the underground room, was cold. She called his name again as she turned on the overhead light. Tj glanced toward the chessboard. The pieces indicated a game had been interrupted in midplay. Odd. As far as she knew, she was the only visitor Zachary ever had. Tj tried the handle connecting the cellar to the main part of the house. It was locked. She knocked and waited several minutes. When no one came, she set her takeout bag on the worktable, went back out through the cellar door, and walked around the outside of the house to the front. She knocked on the front door, but it too was locked. Maybe Zachary had slept in? Then again, maybe he was sick, or he might have fallen and injured himself.

Deciding to risk embarrassing Zachary if she happened to catch him still in bed, she went back around the house and retrieved the key she knew he kept hidden under a rock. She called Zachary's name as she opened the door to the stairway connecting the cellar to the main part of the house and climbed the stairs.

As she inched her way through the kitchen, Tj noticed two takeout containers sitting on the otherwise empty counter. Could Zachary have had another guest to lunch? There were two teacups in the sink. Picking up one of the white Styrofoam containers from The Antiquery, the restaurant her best friend Jenna owned, Tj peeked inside. Clam chowder, Jenna's traditional Friday special, and by the smell of it, the soup had been sitting out since the previous day.

Tj set aside the container and walked toward the large living area at the front of the house. She often wondered about Zachary's life before the accident. Although he'd been nothing more than an eccentric recluse in the fourteen years she'd known him, she'd heard whispers of stories of a young man with movie-star good looks and money to burn who caroused around the countryside looking for short-term relationships with beautiful young girls. Somehow Tj couldn't quite meld that man with the one she knew, but deep in her heart she realized the stories were probably true.

"Zachary?" Tj paused as she entered the large, open living room. Zachary was sitting in his favorite armchair, lifeless eyes staring at nothing in particular. "Oh, God." Tears sprang to her eyes as she ran across the room to Zachary's side. "Zachary?" she cried as she fell to her knees, almost knocking over the table next to the chair. Fighting the nausea that suddenly gripped her, she reached for her cell phone and dialed 911.

"Tj Jensen?" a tall man with eyes even bluer than her own greeted her several minutes later. Must be the new deputy she'd heard about.

"Yes."

"I'm Deputy Dylan Caine, and this is Deputy Long."

"You call in the death?" Deputy Long, a middle-aged man, asked.

"Yes." Tj felt disassociated from the sound of her own voice. Could it possibly be true? Was Zachary really dead?

It had probably only been fifteen minutes since she'd called in the death, but in those fifteen minutes, she'd replayed the scene in her mind time and time again. By the time the deputies had arrived she'd settled into a state of almost catatonic numbness.

"And the reason for your visit?" Deputy Long asked.

Tj stared at the man for several seconds before answering. She wondered where Serenity's usual deputies were, and why this strange man was here in their place.

"Ma'am," the man nudged her impatiently.

"Where are Tim and Roy?"

"Deputy Tim Mathews is out of town for training and Deputy Roy Fisher is home sick. I am on loan from the main office," Deputy Long answered. "Now I'm going to ask you again, what is the reason for your visit?"

"Zachary and I are—*were* friends," she corrected herself because somehow it seemed important.

"What time would you say you got here?" Deputy Long continued.

"About an hour ago. Maybe more." She stared off into the distance. "Actually, probably a little less. Probably thirty minutes," she stammered. "I'm really not sure."

"Maybe it would be best if you sat down," Deputy Caine suggested. "Perhaps on the bench near the front door."

"Yes, I think that would be best." Tj allowed the handsome deputy to take her by the arm and lead her to the bench. He sat down beside her. There was something about him to which she immediately felt drawn. He wasn't drop-dead, supermodel gorgeous the way her new guest Kyle was. He was tall and muscular with blond hair a bit too long to be regulation, a rugged jaw, and a small scar zigzagging across his forehead. Still, it wasn't his smile or adorable dimple that held her attention, but the depth of knowing and compassion in his eyes as he offered her comfort.

"Can I get you anything?" the man asked. "Some water? I think I have an unopened bottle in the car."

"No, thanks, I'm fine. It's just so—" Tj's voice was choked with emotion "—surprising. So very, very surprising. He seemed fine the last time I saw him. Is he? Did he?" Tj tried to gather her thoughts. "How did he die?"

"We're not sure yet. Most likely a heart attack or another age-related occurrence. These things can come on quite suddenly." Deputy Caine looked at her with kind eyes, his voice sympathetic.

"It looks like the coroner is here," Deputy Long interrupted. "Why don't you head inside and see to the removal of the body while I finish the interview?"

Dylan hesitated, as if reluctant to leave his fragile witness, but in the end he did as Deputy Long suggested.

Deputy Long asked her a few questions, made some notes, then closed his notebook. "Do you happen to know his next of kin?" he finally asked.

"Zachary lived alone." Tj stifled a sob. "He didn't have anyone."

"Did you notice anything out of the ordinary when you arrived?"

"Out of the ordinary?" Tj glanced up at the man. "Do you suspect foul play?"

"Actually, no." He looked up from his notepad, meeting Tj's gaze for the first time. "Standard question."

Tj thought about it. "Not really," she replied.

Deputy Long jotted down a few more notes. "Guess we're done. We may need to get back to you with follow-up questions, but until then you can call this number if you think of anything else." The deputy handed her a business card.

"Thank you." Tj took the card. She stared at it as she tried to get her brain to function well enough to let her know what she was supposed to do now. Finally, she stood up and slipped the card into her pocket.

"Zachary has a cat. Crissy. Can I get her?"

He hesitated as he considered her request. "Sure, I guess so. But don't touch anything else."

Tj returned to the house and began calling for the cat, who was nowhere in sight. She paused as she neared the chair where Zachary had sat. Tj held her hand to her mouth. Zachary was an old man in ill health. She shouldn't be surprised by his passing, yet somehow she was. Tj supposed one could never really be prepared for such an abrupt departure.

Tj looked toward the table again and frowned. A beautifully wrapped gift with her name on it sat next to a card, also with her name on it, and an empty glass. Ignoring the deputy's instructions not to touch anything, she picked up the glass and took a closer look. It smelled of alcohol. Zachary never drank alcohol. Tj suspected that whatever had occurred in his life to turn him into a bitter recluse had to do with alcohol. Scotch, to be specific. Although she hadn't seen him take a drink in the fourteen years she'd known him, Zachary kept a bottle of scotch in a glass case in his dining room. Tj wasn't certain what the significance of that particular bottle was, but he'd once told her he kept it as a daily reminder of past sins.

Tj walked into the dining room. The bottle was missing. She looked around the room, but it was nowhere in sight. Something was definitely going on, something that caused the hair on the back of her neck to stand on end. Why after all these years would Zachary break his vow and take a drink? And even more curious, where was the bottle?

The sound of someone returning to the room prompted her to call out again to Crissy, who she found cowering under the dining-room table. Picking up the frightened feline, she slipped the gift and card Zachary had left for her into her bag, took one last look around, then went out to her car. She fought the barrage of tears that were threatening as she put the car into drive and slowly pulled away from the house. Zachary was a strange friend, and their relationship had been unconventional by anyone's standards, but Tj would miss him.

She wondered who'd arrange for the funeral. Maybe Pastor Dan Kensington of Serenity Community Church? When Whinny Newsome died without any family to see to her final arrangements, Dan had organized volunteers from the church to provide a beautiful service and graveside burial.

Tj pulled over to the side of the road as she approached the far-western border of the grounds. She wiped a tear from her eye as she looked back at the roof of the house, which could barely be seen beyond the trees. She picked up Crissy and cried into her soft fur, grieving for the man who had no heirs to leave the home his grandfather had built. She cried for the man whose funeral would most likely be arranged by well-meaning strangers who didn't even know him. But most of all she mourned the loss of a friend who had meant so much to her for so many years.

CHAPTER 4

After leaving Zachary's, Tj took Crissy home and got her settled into the laundry room with a bowl of kibble and a clean cat box. After letting Echo out for a quick run, she took a hot shower, then changed into a well-worn pair of jeans and a warm cinnamon-colored sweater. She then called The Antiquery in the hope of speaking to Jenna, but Jenna's mother and business partner Helen informed her that Jenna had already left for the decorating party at the community center.

On one hand, the last thing she felt like doing was going to the decorating party where she'd have to pretend everything was okay when it clearly wasn't. On the other, sitting home alone with nothing but the memory of Zachary's lifeless eyes to keep her occupied was more than her fragile emotions could take.

Realizing she wasn't ready to deal with the loss of her friend in a public forum quite yet, she decided to attend the party but not mention his death. She glanced in the mirror and realized her red, puffy eyes would be a dead giveaway that something was wrong. She took out her seldom-used makeup bag and tried as best she could to repair the damage brought on by her grief. A little mascara, a light dusting of a dark-colored shadow, and no one would ever know. Pulling her curly hair into a serviceable ponytail, she plastered on a happy face, grabbed her backpack, and headed into town.

* * *

The community center was alive with a happy energy as volunteers worked together to paint backdrops, hang rubber spiders, and string cobwebs. A large scarecrow with a pumpkin for a head and a scythe in his hand greeted guests as they entered the roped-off lawn area. Tj waved to Frannie Edison, the town librarian, who was supervising a group of children that included Ashley and Gracie as they played tag near a grove of maples brilliant with color. The Pumpkin Festival was an annual event that promised both fun and much-needed revenue. Last year the event brought in over eight thousand dollars for the school. This year they hoped to do even better.

"Jen around?" Tj forced a smile as she greeted the school principal, Greg Remington, who was busy rigging up some sort of mechanical arm.

"In the graveyard making tombstones." Greg nodded toward the realistic-looking graveyard set up at the entrance to the building. "Things are really coming together. I think this might be our best haunted house yet. Listen, did you get the schedule of this winter's cross-country meets I left in your box?"

"Yeah, thanks. I'll make copies and hand it out to the girls on Monday."

"Brittany Baxter came in to talk to Sheila yesterday," Greg said, referring to his wife, the high school counselor. "Seems Brittany may have to drop off the ski team this year. Her parents are going through a tough divorce and she might stay with her aunt while they work things out."

"She mentioned that. Poor thing. This breakup has been really hard on her. I thought I'd talk to her next week to see if there's anything I can do to help her get through this. I understand her parents might need their space right now, but

I'm not sure sending her away and disrupting her whole life is the best solution. She needs a stable routine and the support of her friends."

"I agree. Sheila is going to talk to her parents about letting her stay with a friend instead of going to her aunt's. I'll let you know what happens."

"Please do." Tj forced a smile. "I'm going to find Jen and help make tombstones."

"Everything okay?" Greg looked up from the arm he was working on for the first time.

"Why do you ask?"

"It's just that you look sort of—" The principal hesitated, then said, "Never mind. You look great, as always. Don't forget, we still need to talk about your adjunct assignment for the year."

"I know. I'll stop by on Monday," Tj promised as she trotted away with a bounce to her step that she wasn't quite feeling.

Tj found Jenna in the graveyard, knee-deep in tombstones. As an additional fundraiser, members of the community could purchase a tombstone to be painted with a colorful epitaph for a friend or family member. The inscriptions were usually silly in nature, but three years earlier Paul Wright had used his tombstone to propose to Lauren Banks, and a new trend of using the tombstones to relay congratulations and heartfelt messages had been born.

"I heard what happened." Jenna set down the tombstone she'd been painting, stood up, and hugged her best friend. "Dennis was at the station when the 911 call came through. His unit didn't respond since a paramedic was not requested, but he heard everything over the radio. Once he realized the victim was Zachary he called me and let me know what was going on. I'm really sorry. I know you were close. I can't imagine how it must have felt to find him that way."

"Thanks, but I'd rather not talk about it right now. What do you need me to do?"

"I feel like I have a handle on the tombstones but would you mind going over to the school and giving this to Harriet?" Jenna pulled a piece of paper out of her pocket. "It's a list of the cookies I've agreed to donate for the snack bar. She said she'd be working in the cafeteria today."

"Sure, no problem."

Tj took Jenna's list and headed toward the school. The wind had picked up, sending showers of yellow aspen leaves cascading to the ground. The combination of cooling air and the dark clouds hanging over the summit indicated that a storm was on the way. Not that Tj really minded. It had been a dry summer and they could use the rain. She just hoped its arrival wouldn't put a damper on the upcoming festivities.

Entering the cafeteria, she waved at the group of volunteers who were hanging streamers and taping paper ghosts to the walls. The long tables where the student body gathered for lunch were covered with the various supplies that would turn the room into a fall wonderland. Tj could still remember having school lunches on those very tables. Blue plastic trays divided into three sections and filled with cafeteria delights like hamburger gravy, cheesy pasta, and hot dogs on a stick had lined the tables on both sides on any given afternoon. Due to budget cuts and worn-out appliances, the trays had been replaced by boxed lunches prepared by a local restaurant, and the ancient kitchen was now used exclusively for community events.

"I have Jenna's cookie list," Tj said as she walked into the kitchen and handed the paper to Harriet Kramer, Mayor Wallaby's secretary, who had pulled her head out of the cupboard she was stocking.

"Fantastic." Harriet paused to look at the list. "Oh, good,

oatmeal butterscotch chews. My favorite. Is Maggie's Hideaway donating the meat for the barbecue again this year?"

"Probably," Tj answered vaguely. "I'll have to check with my dad. It seems like we donated the patties for the hamburgers and the precooked meat for the barbecue beef and pulled pork sandwiches last year. I'm sure he's planning to do something similar this year."

"If you could ask him and give me a call, that would be great. I'm sure most folks are planning to donate to the snack bar, but so far I only have confirmations from a few of our more organized volunteers. It's been a real struggle to track everyone down this year. I finally managed to reach Kurt Brown at the bowling alley last night to get Alice's list for the beverage shack."

"I heard Alice was out of town."

"Her sister had back surgery. Alice went to help out and won't be back till next week. Kurt had been carrying the list around in his wallet ever since Alice asked him to drop it off over a week ago, so at least one crisis has been averted. If I can get confirmation on the meat, we'll be in business."

Tj pulled out her cell phone and looked at the display. "There's no service in here, but I'll find a better place to give my dad a call and let you know. I can't believe the festival is next week already. It seems like we were just building floats for the Patriot's Day parade."

"I still have the leftover lumber from the town's float in my garage," Harriet confirmed. "I mentioned it to Kurt when I saw him last night, but he was driving his new car so he couldn't pick it up."

"Kurt got a new car?"

"Red convertible," Harriet tut-tutted. "Now you know I'm not one to talk"—Harriet was the second-biggest gossip in town next to Jenna's mother Helen and everyone knew it—"but from what I've heard, Kurt and Alice are months behind on all their local tabs. Not that it's any of my business, mind you, but it seems irresponsible to buy a new car when you owe so many folks so much money." Harriet leaned in and lowered her voice. "Between you and me, I think there might be more to Alice's trip than it would appear."

"I thought you just said her sister had surgery."

"That's the story. I just find it curious that the very day Alice flies out to care for her poor, injured sister, Kurt makes such a large, totally impractical purchase. Not that I'm accusing Kurt of any wrongdoing, mind you." Harriet paused for emphasis. "I'm just saying."

Tj assured Harriet she'd call after speaking to her dad, then removed herself from the conversation. It was probably the best idea she'd had all day. She'd been the topic of the daily tell-all a time or two and knew the experience was less than pleasant. Still, she supposed gossip was as much a part of small-town life as apple pie, community picnics, and Sunday church services. If one chose to live in a small community, it was best to accept the good with the bad.

After helping decorate for a couple of hours, Tj, Jenna, and the girls headed to dinner at Rob's Pizza, a comfy joint with vinyl booths, red-checkered tablecloths, team pictures on the walls, video games, and the best pizza west of the Rockies. The gang filed into a booth in the corner.

The place was packed as usual, and Tj knew almost everyone there. Most nights she would have enjoyed chatting with the Caldwell sisters or the guys from Chamberlain Construction, but the hollowness she felt tonight made her dread the idea of small talk.

"Can we go play video games?" best friends Ashley and Kristi asked on cue.

"Sure, but stay together and don't make a lot of noise. There are people in the restaurant who are actually here to eat." Tj handed each of the girls a couple of dollars. "And keep an eye on Gracie and Kari."

Tj began to relax as she watched the girls trot away. Besides the fact that he made the best pizza around, Rob provided a cozy atmosphere with a lived-in, hometown feel. Somewhat off the beaten path, the eatery catered to locals rather than tourists, as many of the restaurants on the main drag were known to do. The walls were covered with photos of citizens going about their daily lives, winning contests, and receiving awards. As were all the businesses in Serenity, Rob's was dressed in holiday fare, from jack-o'-lanterns sporting goofy grins and lopsided eyes lining the bar to the life-size Frankenstein monster that greeted patrons as they entered the restaurant.

"Ready to talk about it?" Jenna asked after Tj had given their order to the waitress.

"I don't know. Maybe."

"I didn't know Zachary well, but I know you cared about him," Jenna offered.

"I know he was an ornery cuss, but I'm really going to miss him. When I first met him, he'd curse and complain about everything from the weather to the clothes I wore and the noise I made when I chewed my gum, but then he'd spend hours coming up with these games we'd play. My favorites were the puzzles he'd construct for me to solve that got harder and harder each time. I know that most everyone thought my relationship with Zachary was odd but the more I got to know him the more I began to see something different in his eyes—a glimmer of laughter and merriment that I know he tried to hide from the world. I think underneath the gruff exterior he was a good man who'd lived a painful life."

"I'm sorry." Jenna grabbed her hand across the table. "I know it hurts to lose a friend. Is there anything I can do?"

There really wasn't anything Jenna could do, but Tj felt like *she* should be doing something. One of her dearest friends was dead and she was sitting in a restaurant eating pizza. She should call the coroner, or set up an appointment with Pastor Dan to talk about the funeral. Zachary didn't have any family or other close friends to deal with what needed tending to after a loved one passed on.

"I met the new deputy." Tj changed the subject to something a bit less stressful. "He responded to the call today."

"I heard he's a babe."

Tj shrugged. "I guess he's okay."

"I overheard Mom telling Frannie that the guy is a widower with a tragic past."

"Tragic past?"

"I was working the kitchen so I didn't catch the entire conversation, but you know how mom likes to gossip. I'm surprised the poor man's life history hasn't been spread around town by this point. Although, the rumor mill has been pretty busy with speculation about Kurt Brown's new car and what the extravagant purchase might actually point toward."

"Harriet mentioned something about that when I saw her this afternoon."

Jenna leaned in close. "The word around town is that Kurt has hit the wall we most commonly refer to as a midlife crisis. There's even some talk that Alice isn't really helping her sister but has up and left Kurt after his recent string of bad luck."

"You think Alice would leave Kurt over financial issues?"

"Doubtful. But still, it's strange that Kurt would buy a new car on the very day Alice leaves town." Jenna paused. "Oh great, now I'm beginning to sound like my mother, the queen of gossip."

Tj laughed. "You really are. Maybe it's genetic."

"God, I hope not."

"It looks like the pizza is ready." Tj nodded toward the waitress carrying over two large cheese pies. "I'll go get us a glass of wine, you grab the girls."

CHAPTER 5

Later that night, Tj sat on her bed frowning at the beautifully carved puzzle box Zachary had left for her. It wasn't the first time he'd given her such a box. In fact, having to work for a gift by following clues provided in similar puzzle boxes had become an annual game they'd both enjoyed. The problem was that normally he'd provide a clue to get her started.

Traditionally the first clue, once solved, revealed a code that would open the box, which usually contained another clue, which would lead to some small trinket he'd hidden for her to find. While the trinket was usually just something Zachary had laying around the house, the real gift was the fun of the game they shared.

She remembered the first box Zachary had given her. The riddle had been easily solvable, but the clue inside led to a month-long treasure hunt requiring her to track down additional clues he'd hidden in various places around the house. Until then, Tj had viewed Zachary as a lonely old man she'd occasionally visit because she felt sorry for him. But the game had intrigued her, changing their relationship from one based on pity to one based on a common love of games of the mind.

Zachary had taught her so much over the years: how to play chess and solve games of logic, how to both code and decode secret messages using a variety of techniques, how to look at a scene and notice what was odd or what was missing, how to decipher patterns and create hypotheses based on the limited facts he'd put before her. At first, Tj wondered whether Zachary was a highly trained spy. He certainly thought like one, and in her imagination she'd created childhood fantasies of a secret agent hiding out from his past. But as she grew older, she realized he was but a damaged man who had the intelligence to know how to use his imagination to fill his long, lonely days.

Tj sighed as soft jazz played in the background. The pumpkin spice candle on her bedside table filled the room with a seasonal aroma, while a cozy fire danced in the small woodstove her dad had installed in the corner. Crissy, who seemed to have accepted her change in circumstance without so much as a nod, was curled up at the foot of her bed, while Echo lay snoring softly from his napping spot on the rug in front of the raised hearth.

The moment was perfect. On any other night, with the wind whistling through the treetops and the rain pelting the window, she would have enjoyed the cozy feeling of security that comes with knowing the people she loved most in the world were safe and warm inside the sturdy log walls her grandfather had cut and milled himself. But on this particular night her heart was heavy as she stared at the box Zachary so lovingly carved but never had the opportunity to give her. He'd been so excited about the game. More so this time than usual. He'd indicated that the game they were to play was in some way different, more important, than others they'd shared.

"What ya doin'?" Gracie stood at the open door in her fuzzy footie pajamas holding Mr. Mops, the stuffed bunny she'd received last Easter.

"Shouldn't you be in bed?" Tj glanced at the clock, which read 11:42.

"I woke up and heard banging."

The tree outside Gracie's room was probably hitting the wall from the strong wind. When she was her sister's age, she'd try to be brave during thunderstorms, but she'd end up sneaking down the hall to her dad's room and climbing under the covers. He'd pretend to be sleeping, but he always shifted so she could cuddle up next to him as he snored away.

"Okay, climb in." Tj pulled back the covers.

"Is that your present?" Gracie looked at the object in Tj's lap.

"Yeah. It's a puzzle box."

"Don't look like a box." Gracie snuggled next to Tj to get a closer look at the cylindrical-shaped object.

"It's a special kind of box," Tj explained. "See how it has these sections with numbers that rotate?" She demonstrated how the box worked as Gracie looked on. "There are four sections and each one has ten numbers, zero through nine. The secret is to figure out the code and line up the numbers just right. Then the box will open and there will be a surprise hidden inside."

"Like a treasure?" Gracie seemed fascinated.

"Exactly."

Tj stared at the box and frowned.

"Something wrong?" Gracie asked.

"My friend who built the box died before he could give me the clue to open it."

"He didn't leave a card?" Gracie wondered.

Of course, the card. She'd set it aside to read later. She picked it up from the bedspread and read it out loud. "For Tj, on our PERFECT day. As my life draws to a close and my days become numbered, I want you to know that you've been my sanctuary in an otherwise dark life."

"What's a sanctary?" Gracie set Mr. Mops aside to make room for Crissy, who had decided to curl up in her lap.

"A sanctuary is someplace that makes you feel warm and safe. A place where you feel happy."

"I feel happy and warm and safe when I'm with you." Gracie leaned her head against Tj's arm.

Tj smiled and pulled Gracie closer. She kissed the top of her curly head and let the scent of the soap and shampoo from her recent bath calm her soul. "I feel happy and warm and safe when I'm with you too, peanut. The luckiest day of my life was when you and Ashley came to live with us."

"Maybe the clue is sanctary," Gracie suggested.

"Good guess, but we only have four numbers to work with and sanctuary has nine letters. We need a word with four letters."

"If the secret is a word, how come he made numbers and not letters on the box?"

"Well, you see, there's a code." Tj tried to figure out how to explain this to a five-year-old. "Like A is one and—"

"B is two," Gracie joined in.

"Exactly." Pretty quick for someone still in footie jammies.

"Can't be a number?" Gracie wondered.

"Sure, I guess." Tj hadn't really considered that. Every other box Zachary had built for her had been opened by discovering the clue and the key that converted letters into numbers. But she supposed it was possible a number was just a number. The word "numbered" on the card appeared to have a line under it. Tj had assumed the mark was just a smudge, but perhaps Zachary was leaving a clue. "I guess it could be someone's lucky number, or maybe a special date."

"Like Christmas?" Gracie suggested.

"Yeah, or a birthday or an anniversary. An anniversary."

She picked up the box and arranged the numbers to read 1031, Halloween and the anniversary of their first meeting. Nothing. Still, Gracie might be on to something with the number idea. Zachary loved numbers. He spent a lot of time teaching her how to solve puzzles dealing with numbers. He used to tell her that numbers were the basic building blocks of the universe, and an understanding of numbers and their relationship to one another was important not just for mathematics, but for science and art as well.

She looked at the card again. "For Tj, on our PERFECT day. As my life draws to a close and my days become numbered, I want you to know that you've been my sanctuary in an otherwise dark life."

"Can I come in?" Ashley was standing in the doorway dressed in a flannel nightgown with a picture of Cinderella on the front. Her long, red hair hung across her face as she curled the toes of her bare feet against the cold of the hardwood floor.

"Storm wake you?" Tj asked as she turned back the quilt on her other side in welcome.

"No, I heard you talking." Ashley climbed into bed and burrowed under the warm covers. Tj realized Ashley was more like her than she cared to admit. Like Ashley, as a child she'd never simply admit to being scared by a storm, which, Tj realized, was how the ritual of her dad pretending to remain asleep while she climbed into his big bed started in the first place. She wrapped the covers around her sister and showed her how the box worked.

"We thought the clue might be in the card," Tj explained.

Ashley picked up the card and read it. "How come perfect has all big letters?"

Tj took the card from Ashley. "I'm not sure. Maybe Zachary was telling me to look for a perfect number."

"Seventy-three," Ashley proclaimed.

"Why that number?" Zachary once had told her that seventy-three was his favorite number, but she was certain she'd never mentioned it to Ashley.

Ashley shrugged and yawned all at once. "I don't know. I just like that number so I guessed it. Can I have a glass of milk?"

"Sure, but then it's off to bed."

"Can Crissy sleep with me?" Gracie asked.

"I don't see why not. You'll need to keep the door closed, though, so she doesn't get out."

"Okay. I don't think I'll be a-scared if she's with me, but maybe we should turn on the night-light just in case."

"I think that would be a good idea. How about you?" she asked Ashley. "Need a night-light?"

Ashley gave her a look. "I'm eight," she reminded her older sister.

"You're right. I don't know what I was thinking." Tj shuffled both girls out the door and down the hall toward their respective bedrooms.

After getting the girls back to bed, Tj went to the kitchen for a glass of wine. Her dad and grandpa had long since gone to bed, so Tj tossed a log on the fire in the cozy living room. Settling onto one of the overstuffed forest green sofas arranged in a giant U in front of the fireplace, she sunk into the cushions and pulled her Grandma Maggie's handmade quilt over her tucked-up legs. The secret to the riddle had to be something findable. Zachary had never given her a clue she couldn't solve. Of course, the answer was probably hidden somewhere in his house. She took a sip of her wine as Cuervo, the alcoholic tomcat she'd adopted two summers ago, jumped up on the sofa next to her.

"To what do I owe this honor?" she asked the testy tomcat, who usually scurried away at the first sign of a cuddle. Tj had rescued Cuervo from a group of frat guys who had been staying in the campground and thought it would be funny to offer the stray a shot of their libation. Unfortunately, the silly cat enjoyed the tequila, and Tj had been struggling to keep him away from the hard stuff ever since. Cuervo let out a single yowl before curling up in a ball with his head in her lap.

In all likelihood, Cuervo was simply jealous of Crissy and therefore establishing his territorial rights. In a day or two he'd probably be back to growling at anyone who wanted to pet him, but for now she'd enjoy his company.

She absently scratched Cuervo's furry orange head and thought about the glass she'd found next to Zachary's chair. She wondered what, if anything, it might mean. And then there was the bottle itself. If Zachary had been alone in the house at the time of his death, where was the bottle from which he drank? It should've been sitting nearby, and it certainly didn't get up and walk away on its own. She remembered the unfinished chess game and the two containers of clam chowder. Someone must have been with Zachary when he took that noteworthy drink. But who? And if Zachary did have a visitor, where was the second glass? Surely he wouldn't pour a drink for himself and not for his guest.

Then there was Lloyd Benson, who'd reapplied for a permit to build his condominiums. The project had been shot down before because of Zachary's refusal to allow him access through his property. Her grandpa had speculated that Zachary might have sold, but Tj knew in her heart he never would. Still, she had to admit Zachary had been acting differently lately. Could Lloyd's project have anything to do with Zachary's strange actions on the final night of his life?

She looked down at the box in her lap. As unlikely as it seemed that the riddle of the puzzle box had anything to do with the mystery of Zachary's death, opening the box was something she had at least a small amount of control over, so she decided to focus her energy there. Ashley's guess of seventy-three as the perfect number was a good one. Maybe Tj had mentioned it to her at some point. Zachary had justified his choice with a long explanation of prime numbers and mirror numbers and star numbers, which she didn't really remember. The problem was that seventy-three only had two digits and she needed four. She tried 7373, repeating the number, and then 7337, in case he was thinking about the whole thing with the mirror. Neither worked. Maybe the answer was in the word itself.

Tj took out a piece of paper and wrote down the alphabet from A to Z, then corresponding numbers from one to twenty-six. She added the numbers corresponding to the letters in the word PERFECT; P-16, E-5, R-18, F-6, E-5, C-3, T-20. The question was what to do with the numbers now that she had them. In a previous game the answer had to do with finding the sum of the numbers. Tj got out her calculator and added them together: 16+5+18+6+5+3+20=73.

Tj stared at the notepad in front of her. Seventy-three was really more of a favorite number than an actual perfect one. Maybe Zachary was playing on her knowledge of seventy-three being his favorite number in order to lead her to an actual perfect number, like six. Tj walked over to her bookshelf where she kept a paperback of logic puzzles she tried to solve when she couldn't sleep. At the back of the book was a list of certain types of numbers used to create logic puzzles, such as prime and perfect numbers.

"8128," she said aloud. "The only four-digit perfect number is 8128."

She turned the sections of the box to the corresponding numbers and it popped open. Inside the box was a piece of paper with a riddle on it: the next clue in the puzzle. The phrase written on the small piece of parchment read:

From the ashes of the past
springs new Life as truths reveal
the penance of A sinner
and the Gift put forth to heal

Tj frowned. She doubted the game Zachary planned for her had anything to do with his death. Still, the theme of the riddle seemed oddly prophetic. The riddle held no meaning for her, but one word from each sentence was capitalized: From Life A Gift. From life a gift? What the heck did that mean?

What she needed, she realized, was a good night's sleep and the fresh perspective of a new day. Taking the last sip of her wine, she checked the fire, turned off all the lights, picked up Cuervo, called to Echo napping by the fire, and crept up the stairs to the sanctuary of her own bed. Tomorrow would be another day. Perhaps she'd find her answers then.

Tj turned off her light and climbed under her heavy down comforter. Cuervo curled into a ball next to her and rested his head on her pillow as she ran her hands through his long, thick fur. The cantankerous old cat started to purr, something he rarely ever did. Maybe, like with Zachary, there was a warm heart beneath the rough exterior after all.

CHAPTER 6

Sunday, October 24

Tj woke the next morning to hot breath on her face and a heavy object across her feet. It wasn't the first time she'd been awakened by Echo's warm doggy breath as he rested his head on the pillow next to hers, but the soft but heavy weight across her feet was new. And then she remembered Cuervo. The cat yawned then screeched when he spotted Echo's head near hers. Hissing and burrowing under the safety of the covers, he curled up in a tight ball and growled his displeasure.

"Come on out and we'll get some breakfast." Tj slid out of bed, pulled her old wool robe on over the thermals she wore, slipped her feet into a pair of knee-high slippers, picked up the grouchy cat, and headed down the stairs. By the smell of bacon wafting its way up the stairs, it appeared that someone, probably Grandpa, was making breakfast.

"Pancakes?" Ben asked as she opened the back door to let Echo out, then settled Cuervo in the laundry room with his breakfast. His six-foot-four-inch frame looked especially charming today in denim jeans and a dark brown cable knit sweater.

"Thanks, but I think I'll stick with coffee. Couldn't sleep." Adding cream to her coffee, she wrapped both her hands around the large mug, decorated with moose antlers, that her dad had brought back from his trip to Maine the previous year. Even with the fire crackling in the old brick fireplace located between the kitchen and the dining area, the room seemed unusually cold this morning.

"Body needs more than coffee in the morning," Ben warned.

"I know. I'll eat something later. Where are Dad and the girls?"

"Your dad grabbed a cup of coffee and headed over to the lodge to check on the new arrivals and the girls are in the den watching cartoons." Ben ran a dish rag over the deep green tiles of the ceramic countertop while he waited for the pancakes to turn a golden brown. "Helen called earlier. She's taking all the girls to a movie this afternoon. My truck is in the shop, so Doc is coming by to pick me up in an hour or so. I told Helen we'd drop the girls off at her place on our way out to Bookman's. Oh, by the way, someone from the sheriff's office called. He wondered if you could stop by later, at your convenience, of course. He said that it wouldn't take long since Zachary's death was due to natural causes and there wouldn't be an investigation, but he still needed you to fill out some routine paperwork."

"Must have been Dylan." Tj finished her first cup of the rich blend her dad had specially prepared for the resort.

"Dylan?" Ben asked as he grabbed the coffeepot and headed toward the table.

"Deputy Caine." Tj held out her mug for Ben to top off. "Took Clark Leighton's place after he retired."

"I wrote down the name on the pad by the phone, but Caine sounds right." Ben walked across the room, picked up the pad, and handed it to Tj before returning to the stove, scooping the pancakes off the grill, and pouring a generous helping of syrup over the top.

"Okay thanks. I'll go by later this morning."

An hour later, Tj was heading out the door to grab a file she'd left in the lodge as a shiny red '57 Chevrolet with white vinyl seats and chrome wheels pulled into the private drive next to the house. A man of average build with a few extra pounds around the middle, dressed in a red-and-white Hawaiian print sweatshirt and perfectly pressed khakis, waved as he opened the door and climbed out. Pulling up the hood of his sweatshirt to protect his full head of white hair from the rain still pelting the area, he made a mad dash to the covered deck.

Doc, a retired coroner, was portly with a booming voice and a jolly disposition. He tended to do things in a big way, whether it be the clothes he wore, the heartiness of his voice, or the boom of his laughter as he chuckled at his own dumb jokes. He was a friendly sort who more often than not was apt to strike up an in-depth conversation with total strangers in line at the grocery store or lounging on the beach. After moving to Serenity, he'd quickly earned a reputation as a flirt, albeit a debonair and charming one.

"Hey darlin'." Doc wrapped Tj in a wet hug and kissed her on the cheek. "Ben around?"

"He should be down in a minute."

"Ben told me about Zachary. Anything I can do to put some sparkle back in your eye?"

"Actually there is." Tj took Doc's arm and led him into the living room where there was a blazing fire. "Roy and Tim are both out this week, so the new deputy, Dylan Caine, and a substitute, Deputy Long, responded yesterday. Deputy Caine left a message with grandpa this morning asking me to come in to fill out some paperwork. I guess he is convinced we are looking at death by natural causes, so they don't plan to open an investigation."

"And you don't agree?"

"I'm not sure. On one hand there didn't appear to be any sign of foul play, but there was a glass on the table next to the chair where I found Zachary's body. I think it contained scotch, but Zachary never drank. I mean, he religiously never drank. The whole thing seems odd to me. It might be nothing, but I want to be sure. I was wondering if you'd call in one of those favors Sheriff Boggs owes you and see if you can take a look at the body?"

A retired Los Angeles County coroner, Doc worked on an on-call basis with the Paradise County coroner. "Means a lot to you?"

"It really does."

Doc stopped to consider her request. "Guess it couldn't hurt to have a conversation with our good sheriff."

Tj hugged the sixty-two-year-old man. "Thanks, Doc."

Tj shook the rain from her umbrella as she walked into the lobby of the lodge. Maggie's Hideaway was crowded as guests gathered around the pine tables or curled up on one of the sofas in front of the floor-to-ceiling fireplace to read a book, play cards, or work on one of the jigsaw puzzles provided by the resort. Tj picked up the file she was looking for and started toward the front door when she heard her name. She spotted Maude who waved her over to a table where she was playing cards with Millie and Abe and Andy Farmer, the brothers who rented the cabin next to the sisters. If coy smiles and sly glances were any indication, it appeared Maude and Millie had done what they set out to do.

"How can I help you?" Tj walked over to the group, a smile on her face.

"I was wondering if you could help settle a dispute."

"I'd be happy to try."

"Sister and I found a book with an old photo of several men and women ice skating on the lake, but the boys swear the photo must be a fake since the lake is too deep to freeze over. We were wondering if you could tell us which of us is correct."

"Actually you both are," Tj informed them. "The lake is made up of both a large body of water and several isolated coves and fingers. The main body of water never freezes, but many of the bays do, providing both skating and ice fishing in the winter."

"Sounds dangerous," Abe said.

"Can be. The bay to the north of the resort is monitored and maintained, but I wouldn't wander out onto ice that hasn't been checked for depth. Every now and then we have someone fall through. I remember this one time—" Tj paused when she noticed the necklace around Millie's neck: a golden ring with a delicate cross in the center. "That necklace you're wearing—a friend of mine has one just like it."

Millie put her hand to her chest. "It's a fidelity necklace. It's given to select female members of the religious group Sister and I were raised in when they reach their sixteenth birthday. It's a symbol of fidelity to the church above all else. Those who are gifted with the necklace are encouraged to devote their lives to service to the church. Sister has one too."

"Service to the church?"

"The group believed they would become stronger through

structured family units," Maude explained. "Gifted young women were chosen to join these family units, either to produce offspring or provide service through acts of labor such as cooking, cleaning, and caring for the children. Millie and I chose the latter."

"It's a lifetime commitment?"

Millie joined in. "Ideally, yes. It wasn't until our papa died and the group disbanded that Maude and I were released from our commitment, thus allowing us to seek other relationships."

"And other women also stayed?" Tj couldn't believe anyone would give up their life for something chosen for them when they were only sixteen.

"While most who were chosen stayed, there were a few women over the years who chose to leave," Maude said. "Maybe your friend was a member at one time. A member who chose to leave."

"My friend was a man," Tj clarified. "Zachary Collins. Do you know him?"

Tj watched Maude's face carefully. "Name doesn't ring a bell. I guess if you're really curious about the necklace, you can ask him where he got it."

"I'm afraid he's passed on," Tj said. "Just a couple days ago, in fact."

"Oh, I'm sorry to hear that," Millie said sincerely.

Tj spoke to the group for a few minutes longer, then headed out for her appointment with Deputy Caine.

CHAPTER 7

The Serenity branch of the Paradise County sheriff's department was no more than a small brick building tucked behind the county offices. Being a satellite office, the building contained a single holding cell, which was utilized only until a suspect in custody could be transported to the larger jail in Indulgence for booking and lockup. The reception area was little more than a tiny square room with an L-shaped counter, behind which was a desk with a handheld radio and a wall of file cabinets. Small windows placed high on the wall let a modest amount of light into the otherwise drab room.

"Can I help you?" the receptionist, asked.

"I'm here to see Deputy Caine. He's expecting me."

"Have a seat and I'll see if he's available." The woman gestured toward a row of plastic chairs along one of the dingy gray walls before getting up and heading down the narrow hallway.

Tj wandered over to the seating area but remained standing as she stared out the small window, fogged from the warm air inside. She traced a small heart in one corner, an impulse she'd often given into as a child, before quickly erasing it and taking a seat. The room was truly depressing. Grayish walls were cluttered with hastily taped wanted posters, many of which had yellowed with age.

"Deputy Caine will see you now." The receptionist reentered the room. "Last door on the left."

Tj headed down the hall past the holding cell, as well as offices she knew were used by Tim and Roy when they were on duty.

"Ms. Jensen." Dylan stood up as she entered the room, causing Tj to focus not on his adorable smile but on the girth of his chest and shoulders. She'd forgotten how stunning he looked in his perfectly pressed uniform. She wondered if he had them sent out or ironed them himself. "Thank you for coming. Please have a seat."

Tj sat on one of the chairs across from his desk. In direct contrast to the outer office, Dylan's personal space appeared clean and comfortable.

His desk was not only neat and organized, it had been personalized with a macaroni-decorated pencil holder that she imagined had been constructed in someone's first-grade classroom. Alongside the pencil holder was a photo of a beautiful brunette woman with a smile in her eyes. Tj remembered that Jenna had heard that Dylan was widowed. She couldn't help but wonder if the woman in the photo had been his wife.

Beside his desk was a bookcase with a variety of manuals organized by size. Atop the highest shelf sat variegated ivy—real by the look of it—and a photo of a Husky sitting on a large rock with a view of what looked like an Alaskan landscape in the background.

On the second shelf down was a picture of a seemingly happy and carefree Dylan with a young boy on his shoulders, both shirtless at the beach. Dylan was jogging toward whoever had taken the picture, arms raised in victory, as were those of the child he carried.

"Deputy Long has been called back to Indulgence, leaving the task of completing the paperwork regarding Zachary Collins's death to me," Dylan began. "I'll need you to sign your witness statement. Will you read through it first to make certain everything is accurate?"

Tj took the report he handed her and skimmed through the transcription of her interview with Deputy Long, which she barely remembered. Tj had lost people she loved before, but the shock of seeing Zachary's lifeless body had been more than her mind could initially process.

"Will there be an autopsy?" Tj looked up from the report.

"No. In cases of natural death of elderly individuals, we usually find it unnecessary."

"What if the death wasn't natural?"

"You know something we don't?" Dylan asked.

"It's more of a feeling that things weren't quite right. I know that sounds insane given the circumstances, but there were some oddities that keep nagging at me."

"Such as?"

"There was a glass on the table that smelled like it had contained alcohol. Zachary never drank. And there was evidence that Zachary had a visitor prior to his death. There were two takeout containers in the kitchen and two tea cups. Zachary never had visitors."

"Didn't you say that you were there to visit on the day you found him?"

"Well yes, but I was the only visitor Zachary ever had."

"I can understand your concern about the death of your friend but we'll need more than an empty glass and two takeout containers in order to reopen a case which has already been closed."

"I understand." Tj handed over the signed statement and

stood up. "It was nice talking to you. I understand you're new in town. If you need someone to show you around, let me know."

Dylan looked surprised by her offer. "Thanks. I might just do that."

After returning to her car Tj checked her messages. There were two texts: one from Ben, asking if she'd pick up his prescription from the drugstore, and the other from Doc, letting her know Sheriff Boggs had agreed to let him take a look at the body. Initial tests indicated that at the time of his death Zachary had sedatives in his system, but not a trace of alcohol. Doc said he would send a blood sample to a guy he knew, who promised to have a complete toxicology screen back to him within a couple of days.

Tj frowned. Sedatives? Why would Zachary be taking sedatives? And why would he open a bottle of scotch he had been saving for over sixty years but not take a single drink? And if he hadn't drunk from the glass on the table next to the chair, who had?

Grabbing her umbrella, Tj darted out into the pouring rain and dashed into the brightly lit interior of the pharmacy. After buying the pharmacy the new owner had completely remodeled the place, turning a functional but drab store into an inviting shop with old-fashioned appeal.

"Hey, Tj." The new owner, David Harris, smiled at her from behind the counter. His brilliant white and perfectly pressed lab coat covered slacks and a sharply pressed dress shirt. "Here to pick up your grandpa's prescription?"

"He told me it was ready."

"Just give me a minute and I'll get it."

While David headed to the backroom, Tj wandered around

the cozy shop, pausing to smell one of the candles on display. Cinnamon. It made her think of the cinnamon toast Zachary used to make for her when she was younger. Setting the candle down, Tj walked to the counter as David came to meet her. Crossing her arms on the shiny surface, she said, "I guess you've heard about Zachary Collins?"

"I have. It's a damn shame."

"Zachary and I were good friends so I asked Doc to look into things for me. Doc informed me that at the time of his death Zachary had a sedative in his system. I was wondering if you could tell me if he'd bought anything from you."

David thought for a moment before answering. "I sent blood-pressure medication up to his place once a month, but other than that he hasn't filled any prescriptions in quite a while."

"I know he had a hard time sleeping. Did he order any sleeping aids recently?"

"I don't think so, unless he got them over the counter."

Tj frowned. "Okay, thanks. Just put Grandpa's medication on our account." She picked up the small white pharmacy bag. Zachary never went out, so the odds of his buying anything over the counter were minimal. However, he did have groceries and supplies delivered to his home once a week, so it was possible he'd bought an over-the-counter sleeping aid from the general store. If he had, chances are there would be evidence of this in his home.

Tj had plans to go to Jenna's for lunch, but first she wanted to stop by Zachary's, so she texted Jenna and told her that she might be a few minutes late. A quick trip out to Zachary's really wouldn't take that long and it might help to ease her mind of the nagging suspicion that was beginning to develop.

*   *   *

Driving through the wrought-iron gates and heading toward the house for the first time since she had discovered Zachary's body left Tj with a nervous feeling in the pit of her stomach. She paused and looked at the house. Every window was shuttered, which gave visitors the deliberate impression they were not welcome at the once stately manor.

Tj parked her car around back, then let herself in through the cellar door. The house was as it always was, dark and musty with a penetrating silence that seemed to pull you into its hollowness. Tj understood that hollowness, the cavern that remained when the very light of your life had been taken away. Tj had been a child when her mom deserted her, old enough to feel the void of her absence but not to understand the why and the how.

By the time she was in elementary school her mom would pop into town for brief and uncomfortable visits that only lasted until her mother satisfied any maternal instincts she might have been experiencing. Once her urge was satisfied, she'd leave again in order to move on to the next man as well as the next thrilling adventure in her life.

Tj stopped to listen as the old grandfather clock ticked away the minutes. It seemed so odd to be standing alone in the very room where she'd found Zachary's body just the day before. She wondered what had gone through his mind during those final moments. Had he known he was going to die? Had he been afraid, or had he been relieved not to go on living?

Tj knew that if Zachary was taking sedatives to help him sleep they'd most likely be in the bathroom which adjoined his bedroom. She slowly climbed the stairs, placing one foot in front of the other as she made her way up the dark passage. The house felt menacing, with an eerie silence heavy with Zachary's passing.

A quick search of the bathroom resulted in a bottle of aspirin, the blood pressure medication David mentioned, and a jar of antacids. Tj glanced at the bedside table as well as the nearby dresser, both of which were void of any type of medication. Tj knew that, other than the upstairs bedroom and bath, the rooms on the second story had been closed off for quite some time, so she made her way back down the stairs toward the kitchen.

The empty tea cups and half-full takeout boxes were still in the same place that they'd been the previous day. Tj opened and closed the cupboards looking for pill bottles which might contain a sedative but all she found were antique dishes and various canned goods.

After a brief search she came to the conclusion that any medication Zachary possessed had been stored in the upstairs bathroom, which meant that the sedative found in Zachary's system most likely hadn't come from medication he kept on hand. Tj wanted to expand her search but she knew that Jenna was expecting her, so she texted her best friend to let her know she was on her way.

As she made her way back through the living room she paused at the antique hutch to retrieve the necklace she was sure mirrored Maude and Millie's. She took the necklace out of the box and studied it. She had no idea how Zachary had ended up with a necklace which would have been given to a female member of an obscure religious group, but after re-examining the necklace she was sure it was the same as the necklaces worn by the sisters.

*   *   *

"Sorry I'm late," Tj greeted Jenna when she arrived at her home on the river a few minutes later. "I had to stop by and sign some paperwork at the sheriff's office, and then I wanted to stop by Zachary's to check for sedatives."

"Sedatives?" Jenna asked as she took freshly baked bread from the oven and cut it into thick slices.

Tj shared Doc's findings.

"Seems odd. Did you mention the sedatives to the new deputy when you stopped by this morning?"

"No, I found out about the sedatives after I was at the sheriff's office. I guess I can stop back by, although I'm still trying to make up my mind about the guy."

"What do you mean?" Jenna asked as she set the salads she'd prepared ahead of time onto the dining table.

"On one hand, he seems really nice. And compassionate. Unlike the loaner deputy who responded to the 911 call along with him. On the other hand, when I tried to express my concern that the case had been closed without any sort of an investigation, he seemed somewhat dismissive."

"I suppose he is just doing his job. I imagine there are certain protocols for reopening closed cases that must be adhered to."

"Yeah, I guess. Did you ever find out anything more about the man's past from the gossip hotline? He had some photographs in his office that piqued my interest. One specifically of a very beautiful woman with dark hair whom I am guessing might have been his wife."

Jenna poured two glasses of iced tea. "No, I guess the new deputy wasn't as newsworthy as I originally thought. It seems the chatter has died down and the hens have moved on to other topics. If you are really interested, we can Google him."

"Seems like an invasion of privacy."

"Maybe, but anything we find on Google is readily available to anyone who bothers to look."

Tj hesitated. "I guess I am kind of curious."

"Let's eat first," Jenna suggested. "Then we can use my laptop to find out everything there is to know about the cute new deputy in town."

After lunch, Jenna brought her laptop into the kitchen and set it up on the table. She logged on and then typed Dylan Caine into the search engine. "Oh my God," she said when the first article popped up.

"What?" Tj asked.

"Remember that tragic past my mom mentioned?"

"Yeah."

"Well tragic is putting it mildly. Eight months ago someone broke into Deputy Caine's apartment, shot him five times, and then killed his wife right in front of his eyes."

Tj put her hand to her chest. "That's awful. Who would do such a thing?"

"According to the article, which was written just the day after the incident, Deputy Dylan Caine and his wife Anna were shot by a gang member out to seek revenge for the death of a fellow gang member who died from gunshot wounds he received from a standoff the previous week. The reporter who wrote this article believed that Deputy Caine was the target while his wife was simply shot in the crossfire. She died instantly."

Tj's heart bled for the poor man. She couldn't imagine how unbearable it must have been to watch someone you loved die all the while knowing it was most likely your fault. "Did they catch the guy?"

"I don't know what eventually happened, but as of the time the article was published, they had not found the killer." Tj looked over Jenna's shoulder as she returned to the page with the search results. "There is an article covering Dylan's rehabilitation and then another when he returned to the Chicago Police Department for limited duty after he was released from the hospital," Jenna pointed to the screen. "There are a couple of other small mentions regarding his work with the CPD and then a more recent article covering his resignation from the CPD prior to taking the job here." Jenna opened the last article she mentioned.

"Sounds like he quit CPD due to some sort of a disagreement," Tj commented as she read over Jenna's shoulder.

"It does seem that way, although the article really doesn't go into specifics. I guess if you want additional information regarding the shooting you can simply ask Dylan."

"Does the first article mention the name of the shooter?"

Jenna returned to the first article she'd found. "No. It looks like his name was withheld because he was a minor."

Tj couldn't imagine that a kid would do such a horrible thing, but she'd lived at Paradise Lake her entire life and was somewhat sheltered from the rest of the world, where she knew things like this happened every day.

"So how are you doing with your own loss?" Jenna inquired after she logged off. "I know how hard Zachary's death has been for you."

"It's been hard, but I'm dealing. The thing is, I feel like there is more to Zachary's death than meets the eye."

"What do you mean?"

"I checked with David at the pharmacy, and he said Zachary did not have a prescription for sedatives. I then went by Zachary's house and checked in the bathroom as well as the bedroom and kitchen, but the only prescription drugs I found were for high blood pressure. And then there's the scotch."

"Scotch?"

Tj explained about the glass she'd found on the table next to where Zachary died and the fact that the tox screen showed that, although there were sedatives in Zachary's system, there wasn't a drop of alcohol in his system.

"That is odd. So what are you thinking?"

"I'm not sure. At least not yet. I have all these random thoughts floating around in my head but they seem fragmented at this point. I know that Zachary was an old man and could very well have died of natural causes, but my gut is telling me there is more to it."

"If you need anything at all you know you can ask."

"Do you happen to remember who bought takeout orders of clam chowder from you on Friday?"

"Clam chowder?"

"When I arrived at Zachary's house, I noticed two half-eaten takeout containers in the kitchen. The containers were from The Antiquery and they contained clam chowder. I thought I'd track down Zachary's guest and see if he or she could provide any insight into what might have gone on that night."

"It was slow on Friday, so I actually do remember who I sold takeout to: Melanie Jacobs, Mark Highlander, Rita Halliwell, and Jeff Warren."

"I honestly can't imagine why any of the four would have been at Zachary's on Friday, but I guess it couldn't hurt to have a chat with them."

"It seems like a longshot. I can't imagine that any of these people even knew Zachary. Based on what I've observed during the course of your friendship with the man, he was pretty selective about who he spent time with."

"I agree, but someone brought the chowder to Zachary." Tj glanced at the clock on the wall. "Thanks for lunch. I'm sorry I don't have more time to hang out, but I really should get going. I told dad I'd help out at the resort this afternoon. I know he is short-staffed."

CHAPTER 8

As predicted, it had been a busy afternoon with weekend guests checking out and new guests checking in, so by the time everything had been squared away, dinner prepared and eaten, baths given, and sisters tucked into bed, Tj was exhausted. She never had gotten around to following up on the clue relating to the clam chowder but it was late so it would have to wait until the following day.

She turned off the lights and locked the exterior doors as she made her way through the house and up the stairs to her second-story bedroom. The light was still on in her grandpa's bedroom, so she knocked and poked her head in.

Ben sat on the side of his bed looking at an old black-and-white picture of himself, his wife Maggie, for whom the resort had been named, and his son Mike when he was an infant.

"Seems like only yesterday. Time really gets away from you," he said without looking up. "Today would have been Grandma's sixty-fifth birthday."

Tj suddenly remembered the pancakes. Ben made them every year on Maggie's birthday, but Tj had been too self-absorbed that morning to notice. "Oh, Grandpa, I'm so sorry. I totally forgot."

Ben put his arm around Tj's shoulders. "It's okay, pumpkin.

You've had a difficult couple of days, and Grandma has been gone for quite some time."

"Still, I should have remembered." Tj put her head on Ben's shoulder and looked at the photo. "You look really young."

"Never was one for the noise and congestion of the big city. After my dad died I took the money he left me and bought the biggest piece of property I could afford. Figured I'd build a little cabin and live out my life in peaceful solitude."

"And then you met Grandma." Tj had heard this story many times, but it was nice to focus on pleasant memories after the stressful day she'd had.

"She was a feisty little thing. Came to Paradise Lake one summer with her parents who owned one of the big houses on the East Shore. At first we didn't really get along, since all I wanted was to be left alone and she was a five-foot-tall spitfire who insisted on hanging around and giving me advice I didn't want or need."

"By the end of summer you were hopelessly in love," Tj filled in. "And when you told her you weren't ready to return to civilization, she agreed to stay at the lake with you."

"Not many women would have done that. Had a one-room cabin, outdoor plumbing, and a woodstove for heat and cooking."

"You were married in the little church in Serenity, built another room onto the cabin, and a year later my dad was born."

"Best time of my life."

Tj loved the story of how her grandparents had met and started the resort. In her mind it rivaled any fairy tale she'd been told as a child.

They seemed the perfect couple. Her grandfather was tall and strong with a deep voice and quiet authority that everyone in the community respected. But at home it was her grandmother, with her petite frame and fiery disposition, who ran the show.

"After Dad was born you used the money Grandma's mother left her and built the resort. First the campground and a little one-room restaurant, and then the cabins, the marina, and the Lakeside Bar and Grill. And later, the larger house and general store."

"Figured your grandma gave everything up to live with an ornery recluse like me, least I could do was build her a nice home."

"You built her more than a home." Tj kissed her grandpa's cheek. "You built her a legacy. One that you've passed down to Dad, and someday he'll pass on to me."

"She was quite a woman."

"That she was." Tj thought about her grandmother, how much she'd loved her and how empty her life had seemed after she passed. "I really miss her."

"Me too." Ben hugged Tj. "She's been gone a long time, but there are still moments when I feel like I can hear her laugh or smell the scent of that fancy perfume she loved so much. Guess there are memories that live on, no matter how many years pass."

Ben and Tj sat together for several minutes, remembering the woman they both loved, before Ben eventually asked, "Haven't really had a chance to talk to you about your friend Zachary's death. Are you okay?"

Tj sighed. "I'm okay. It's just that everything seemed so sudden. In some ways the whole thing doesn't seem real. It's like my mind hasn't accepted the fact that he's gone. I keep thinking, 'I have to tell Zachary about that,' and then I remember."

"It's like that at first. I remember when your grandma passed. For weeks afterward, in those first few seconds after I woke up in the morning, I'd forget she was gone. I'd expect to see her lying next to me. And then I'd remember, and the grief would be almost unbearable. I know it's hard now, but it gets better."

"I hope so. Did you know Zachary before?" she asked.

"Before he locked himself away in that big old house?" Ben clarified.

"Yeah, before the accident."

"No," Ben answered. "By the time I moved to the lake he had already settled into a life of seclusion. Most folks don't really understand why a man would cut himself off like that. They figured it had something to do with the scars on his face. Heard a man died in that accident. Still, to cut yourself off like that seems a bit extreme. Although I guess if you're going to live a life of isolation, Paradise Lake is the place to do it."

Tj thought about the isolated bay and huge mansion surrounded by old-growth pines where Zachary had lived. Just to the left of the mansion was an unobstructed view of the cascading waterfall where Paradise River emptied into the lake. The scenery within the spectacular private estate was awe inspiring, but to spend sixty years in isolation?

"Bookman once told me he'd thought of basing one of his characters on Zachary," Ben informed her. "Said he was fascinated by the idea of a man living within the confines of a self-constructed prison when there was so much beauty just outside his door. Personally, I find the whole thing a bit less fascinating and a bit more tragic."

"I agree with you. By the way, we have a guest who wants to meet Bookman."

"Chap by the name of Kyle?"

"You've met him?"

"At the bar the other night. Nice young man. Was sitting

alone eating a bucket of chicken wings, so I stopped to say hi. Chatted for a bit, then he offered to help me decorate for the party. Mentioned he met you and Echo."

"Echo decided to introduce himself. We talked for a few minutes. He's in town for a job interview."

"Be a welcome addition."

"I guess. He said he was interviewing with a company called the Repository. Have you ever heard of them?"

Ben thought about it. "Can't say I have. Thinking about a hot chocolate. Care to join me?"

"Love to."

CHAPTER 9

Monday, October 25

Serenity High School and Serenity Elementary School had been built on the same plot of land, with a common library, administration office, and cafeteria. Large beige buildings with multiple wings and indoor walkways had been laid out in a pattern Tj likened to a giant spider caught in a web. The school district had implemented a late-start schedule due to the inclement weather, but even with that Tj found it hard to focus. After walking the girls to their classrooms on the elementary side, she'd headed through the maze of hallways toward the teacher's lounge in the high school. She poured herself a cup of coffee, then sat down next to Nikki Weston, a history teacher. Nikki wore her dark brown hair chin length with thick bangs that almost covered her eyes. Fair skin, a tendency toward pudginess, and studious glasses made her look a lot like Velma from the *Scooby-Doo* cartoons.

"New hobby?" Tj asked. She was filling out an application for an after-school bowling league.

"New club," Nikki corrected. "It looks like I've been

appointed teacher rep, even though I don't know the first thing about bowling."

Tj cringed. "I heard there were a bunch of new clubs on campus."

"That consultant Greg hired to help us qualify for more grant money recommended the school expand its extracurricular activities as a way to demonstrate a broader diversification. The only two choices left by the time he called me into his office for this year's adjunct assignments were bowling and choir. I'm not a big fan of bowling, but I feel sorry for the poor sap who ends up with choir."

Tj had a sick feeling she knew exactly who that sap was going to be. She'd blown off the first meeting Greg had set to discuss her adjunct assignment in favor of attending an out-of-area football game. Had she known choir was going to be the only choice left by the time she got around to rescheduling that meeting, she might have decided otherwise. Oh, well. It had been a good game, and the Serenity Black Bears had won in overtime. How bad could choir really be?

With today's late start, the normal fifty-minute periods had been reduced to thirty minutes. It was doubtful Greg would get to her today. Maybe by the time they had their meeting, all the adjunct assignments would be taken and she'd just have to provide refreshments for the annual open house like she had the year before.

Nikki frowned as a streak of lightning lit up the dark sky. "I was planning to take this application over to the bowling alley during my prep, but with this weather I may just wait."

"It's really coming down out there. They closed Highway 28 due to flooding. I'm willing to bet there will be a lot of absent students. I don't think I'm even going to have my girls dress. It looks like another hangman tournament in the making."

"I'd already decided to do a study hall today. Mock trials are next week, so I had planned to have Glen Keller come in to discuss courtroom etiquette and procedure," she said, referring to the town's only resident attorney, "but I ran into him at Fuze on Saturday night and he said he had to reschedule." Nikki taught junior and senior history and was known for her penchant to teach through role-playing. "I didn't have time to come up with another lesson plan so I figured I'd let the kids study for next week's exam."

"You went to Fuze?"

Nikki blushed. "You know how Carl has been bugging me to go out with him for months?"

Carl Osgood, the incredibly handsome varsity football coach, had decided Nikki was a perfect match for him and had been campaigning to take her out since school started in September. Nikki made it clear from the beginning that they had nothing in common and he should move on to someone else. Her continued refusal to date him, however, seemed only to make him more determined to win her over.

"You didn't?"

"I did," Nikki admitted. "Mostly to get him off my back. I figured one disastrous date and he'd leave me alone."

"And did he?"

"Not exactly. We had a fantastic time. We're going out again on Saturday."

Nikki was a wonderful person, but much more of a curl-up-on-the-sofa-with-a-good-book type than a dance-the-night-away-at-a-loud-club girl. In fact, Tj had never known her to do much of anything on a Friday or Saturday night, unless the opera was in Reno or she and Jenna invited her to movie night at the resort.

"Yeah, but Fuze?" Tj couldn't help repeating it.

"I know. I thought I'd hate it, but it was fun. I wouldn't want to do it every night, but maybe once in a while. I mean, if someone as stodgy as Glen Keller can party the night away, I certainly can."

Nikki had a point. While Glen was well known in the community as a competent attorney, he was a timid mouse of a man. And his wife, Marjorie, was the last person she'd expect to see in a club with half-naked women dancing in cages. Tj wasn't sure how Glen had wound up with a wife who was built like a linebacker and had a personality to match, but she suspected it had something to do with money. Marjorie had it and Glen liked to spend it.

"Was Marjorie with him?" Tj asked.

"No, he was alone. Guess he's a regular at the casino. Carl said he once saw Glen drop ten grand in one night."

"Ten grand? Where would he get that kind of money?" Marjorie had come into a large sum of money when her father died, and Glen seemed to do okay for himself as the town's only attorney. They lived in a large house on the lake and drove the newest imports. But still...ten grand in one night?

Nikki shrugged. "No idea. Maybe he has a money tree in his backyard."

"I hope you're right. If he's gambling away Marjorie's inheritance, she's going to kill him."

Later that morning, Tj sat in her office looking at the pile of paperwork she'd been pushing around for the last hour. She knew she'd regret it later if she let herself get behind, but the more she tried to concentrate on soccer lineups and ski-meet schedules, the more she found her mind drifting to thoughts of Zachary and his unexplained death. If she was going to convince

Dylan to reopen the case open, she was going to have to come up with a concrete reason for him to do so.

She knew she needed to focus on her job, but she found herself dialing the number for Rita's Roses. Of the four names Jenna had given her the previous day, Tj knew Rita Halliwell the best.

Rita owned one half of a local enterprise known as Guns and Roses, an interesting shop which sold guns and roses. The enterprise, which had originally been owned by Rita's dad and sold guns and ammo, had taken on a new personality when Rita's father died and Rita wanted to sell flowers in her half of the shop she'd inherited along with her brother Brandon.

"Hey, Rita."

"Can you hang on just a sec?" Tj could hear the sound of people talking in the background.

"Sure, no prob." Tj twisted one of her auburn curls around her finger and listened to the hold music as she waited.

"Sorry," Rita said. "Olivia was here to pick up the bouquets for her dinner party." Olivia Wallaby, the mayor's wife, loved to talk.

"I called to ask about the clam chowder you bought from The Antiquery on Friday."

"What about it?"

"Did you happen to have dinner that night with Zachary Collins?"

"No. Brandon and I ate the chowder while we watched a movie and discussed the sad state of affairs where neither of us had a date on a Friday night. Why?"

Tj briefly explained about her desire to find the person who had shared Zachary's last meal in the hopes of answering the lingering questions that were occupying her mind.

"I heard Zachary had died. I'm sorry. I know you were

close. If I hear of anything that might help you find the answers you are looking for I'll be sure to let you know."

"Okay thanks. I'll talk to you later."

Tj stared out the window after she hung up. As unlikely as it seemed, Melanie, Jeff, or Mark had to have dined with Zachary on the night of his death, and she intended to find out which was the one to share his last meal.

"Something wrong?" Greg Remington poked his head into the door of her tiny office.

Tj shifted her gaze and forced a smile. "Why do you ask?"

"For one thing, you were staring out the window with a scowl on your face; for another, you're late for our meeting."

Tj glanced at the clock on the wall. The grant-writing meeting was supposed to start ten minutes ago. "I'm really sorry," she said, gathering her notes. "I've had a lot on my mind."

"Understandable," the principal said. "It's hard to lose a friend. Anything I can help with?"

"Not really." She followed Greg down to the conference room where their meeting was being held.

"I never met Mr. Collins, but my neighbor Jeff Warren spoke highly of him."

Tj frowned. "Jeff knew Zachary?" Tj didn't know Jeff well, but she'd chatted with him a time or two while having work done on her 4Runner.

"Zachary hired Jeff to do some handyman work for him a few years back. Jeff didn't go into detail, but he said the two of them had something in common and hit it off. Seems Zachary gave him the money to open his auto repair shop."

"Really?" In all the time she had known him, Zachary had never once mentioned knowing Jeff Warren. Tj was starting to question how well she really knew her old friend.

"You seem surprised," Greg said.

"I'm having a hard time imagining what the two might have in common. What's Jeff, like twenty-five?"

"Twenty-eight, actually. Seems age isn't a big issue with Mr. Collins. You're only twenty-six and the two of you were friends," Greg reminded her.

"Yeah, I guess."

"By the way, we need to talk about your adjunct assignment for this year. There's only one option left, but it's an exciting one, full of opportunity."

"Serving refreshments at the annual open house is pretty exciting."

"What do you know about choir? Show choir, to be exact."

"I'm afraid I can't sing," Tj said.

"I'm guessing the recruits strong-armed into joining can't sing either, so you'll be in good company." Greg turned the corner and headed toward the conference room. "When Marley first approached me with the idea I was against it, but her father is making a sizeable donation to the school and Marley wants to sing."

"But I already have soccer after school."

"I thought of that. I've asked Carl to cover your fifth period weight training class on Tuesdays and Thursdays. Your first class with your new choir will be tomorrow in room A5."

"Terrific."

CHAPTER 10

After school, Tj dropped the girls at dance class, then decided to drop in on Mark. Her first instinct was to pay a visit to Jeff after the news Greg shared with her regarding Jeff and Zachary's friendship, but when she called his garage she was told Jeff was off the mountain and wouldn't be back until the following day. Chances are that Jeff was the one who brought the clam chowder to Zachary's house, but she reasoned if Zachary could be friends with Jeff without her knowing anything about it, then maybe he was also friends with Mark. After all, Mark delivered propane for the local distributer and Zachary's house was isolated enough so as to require the use of propane for heating and cooking. It only made sense that Mark and Zachary would've run into each other from time to time.

Tj called the company Mark worked for and was told he was off for the day, but the woman who answered the phone assured Tj that most afternoons Mark could be found at Murphy's, the local bar.

Murphy's had been her grandfather's hangout since before Tj was born. Some of her earliest memories were of sitting next to her grandpa at the bar, sipping a soda and watching a game on television. Technically, a five-year-old wasn't allowed to sit at a bar, even in the state of Nevada, but at Murphy's no one stood on formality and law enforcement most often turned a blind eye.

"Hey, Tj, what can I get yah?" Murphy, a first-generation Irish immigrant with a strong accent and an inviting smile, asked when Tj walked in.

"I'm looking for Mark Highlander."

"In the back playing pool."

Luckily Mark was alone in the back room shooting a solo round.

"Wanna play?" Mark asked when Tj entered the room.

"Sure. I have a few minutes."

Mark racked the balls while Tj picked out a cue.

"I guess you heard about Zachary Collins," Tj commented as she waited for Mark to take the first shot.

"Yeah, I heard."

"I know that you delivered propane out to his place every month or so. Did the two of you ever chat?"

Mark laughed as he missed his shot and Tj lined up to take her turn. "The old guy never even poked his head out the door. I'd just show up, fill the tank and leave. I did notice him looking out the window at me a time or two. Why do you ask?"

"I'm trying to find out who dined with Zachary last week on Friday," Tj answered as she began methodically clearing her balls from the table.

"Well it wasn't me. The guy gave me the creeps. Every time I had to go out to his place, I'd start to have flashbacks to every horror movie I'd seen."

"Zachary may have looked like a monster but I can assure you that he wasn't one. In fact, he was a very nice man."

"If you say so. How'd you learn to play like that?" Mark asked as Tj finished off the game.

"My grandpa taught me to play when I was so short I had to stand on a chair to make a shot."

"Another game?"

"Thanks, but I really need to go." Tj paused and turned. "During your routine visits to fill Zachary's tank, did you ever notice if he had any visitors?"

"Just you. Why do you ask?"

"No reason. Have a nice day."

After Tj left the bar she considered whether or not she'd have time to pay a visit to Melanie before she had to pick up the girls. The girls had both tap and ballet today which made for a two-hour class and her stop at Murphy's had been brief, so she figured she'd have time for a quick visit.

Melanie lived in a modest two-story house on Oak Avenue. Overgrown bushes along the front of the chain-link fence provided a privacy shield from the busy street. The front lawn was neatly trimmed but littered with abandoned bicycles, skates, dolls, and various pieces of sporting equipment. Tj hurried through the rain, carefully picking her way through the toy minefield, and climbed the three freshly painted steps to the covered front porch. The sound of children laughing and calling out to each other could be heard through the partially open windows on the second floor.

"Yeah?" A teenage boy with shaggy black hair and a silver nose ring answered the door.

"Hi Troy. I'm here to see your mom." Tj smiled at the boy who was dressed only in boxer shorts and white gym socks.

"Mom," the boy yelled, then walked away, leaving the door open without inviting her in.

"Yeah?" someone called from upstairs.

"Door."

"I'll be right there."

Tj could hear something crash from overhead as she waited. A dog barked, and a door slammed from somewhere at the back of the house. And she thought her life was hectic. Melanie's husband had run off with his secretary the previous summer, leaving her with their six kids. The gossip line had been abuzz as friends and neighbors speculated about how she was going to make it on her own and whether the kids would be shuffled off to various relatives if the poor woman was unable to cope.

"Hi." An adorable little girl with a head of blond ringlets and deep blue eyes came to the door. "Mom's fixing the toilet. Someone—not me—flushed one of Holly's diapers and water leaked all over the floor. My names Delilah. What's yours?"

"Coach Jensen." Tj smiled at the girl in the Strawberry Shortcake t-shirt, who she suspected was indeed the one who had flushed the diaper down the toilet.

"I'm four and a third. How old are you?"

Tj thought for a second. "Twenty-six and a half."

"Delilah, can you let out the dog?" her mom called from upstairs.

"Okay," she called back. "I gotta go." She turned and trotted toward the back of the house where Tj had heard the dog barking.

A tired-looking, middle-aged woman with bags under her eyes and a diaper tossed over her shoulder greeted her at the door. "Hey, Tj. Come on in. I'm sorry Troy left you standing on the porch. His manners vanished the minute he hit puberty. Can I get you something to drink?"

"No, thanks." Tj followed Melanie through the clean, if somewhat cluttered, home as she led her down a hall toward the family room at the back of the house. As she passed the kitchen, she saw a small child, no more than two, sitting alone in a bright yellow high chair.

"Becka," the woman called.

"Yeah, Mom?"

"I have company. Haley's in the tub. Can you get her dressed?"

"Sure, okay," Becka called back.

"Sorry about the commotion. It's been one thing after another today. I decided to let the older kids stay home, with the late start and all. To be honest, I've been regretting that decision all day."

"I can see you're busy." Tj sat on the sofa, unsure how to proceed. "I won't keep you long. It's just that...I guess you heard about Zachary Collins."

"Yes," Melanie confirmed. "I was sorry to hear he passed on."

"This is going to sound weird, but I was wondering if the two of you were friends."

"Friends? No. We spoke a time or two on the phone, but I wouldn't call us friends."

"You spoke on the phone?"

"He'd call from time to time to talk to Glen." Melanie was local attorney Glen Keller's secretary.

"Did Glen know Zachary?"

"Sure. Glen managed his estate."

"Managed his estate?" Tj asked.

Melanie hesitated. "I'm not sure I should be telling you this, but seeing as you were Zachary's friend and the man is dead now, I don't see how it can hurt." Melanie's large gray cat jumped onto the couch and settled into her lap. "Mr. Collins's grandfather put Zachary's inheritance in a trust managed by Glen's grandfather who founded the law firm. Zachary never took control of the estate. I don't claim to have the entire history, but it seems Zachary's father was afraid his wild, irresponsible son was going to drink and gamble away the entire Collins fortune. He had the trust documents changed so that

Zachary had to be thirty, rather than the original twenty-one his grandfather had stipulated when he set up the trust, to gain full control of his assets."

"He could do that?"

Melanie shrugged. "I guess so. I'm pretty sure Zachary's dad controlled the trust until he died when Zachary was in his early twenties. By the time Zachary finally met the age requirement, he was already sequestered in his big old house. When Glen inherited the law firm, he took over as estate administrator."

"Did Glen and Zachary meet often?" Tj asked.

"Not really. Mr. Collins's needs were few, and he didn't seem to care much about the day-to-day management decisions regarding the estate."

"Is it possible Glen and Zachary had a dinner meeting on Friday? I noticed that Zachary had two takeout containers of clam chowder in his kitchen."

"I suppose it's possible but I sort of doubt it. For one thing, Glen hates clam chowder, which I by the way happen to love, and for another, Glen had a big court case last week that kept him pretty busy."

A phone rang and Melanie set the cat on the floor, picking a stray hair from her tan sweater as she moved to answer the call.

"I got it," someone called from upstairs.

"I appreciate your sharing this with me." Tj stood up. "Thanks for your time, and please bring the kids by the Lakeside Bar and Grill for dinner on me. I'll leave a gift voucher at the front desk under your name."

"That's very nice of you. I could really use a night out, but is it okay if I bring a couple of friends and get a sitter for the kids instead?"

"More than okay." Tj hadn't had an adult night on the town

since her sisters had come to live with her, so she could relate. Most Friday nights, she and Jenna and the four girls went to a movie and maybe shared a pizza at Rob's or burgers at the Burger Barn. Not that Tj didn't enjoy spending time with her sisters, but the thought of Nikki dancing the night away at Fuze made Tj realize she seriously needed to add some balance to her life.

After visiting Melanie, Tj still had a little time before she had to pick her sisters up so she decided to drive by Glen's office just in case he was in. If, as Melanie claimed, Glen had managed Zachary's estate, maybe he could provide some insight into what was on Zachary's mind during his final days.

Two years earlier, when the Serenity Business Park was built, Glen had moved his office to the complex, which also housed several other professionals including a doctor, a dentist, and an accountant. Although the architect had done a good job making the building blend in with the natural landscape, Tj didn't think it characterized Serenity's small-town charm. When Lloyd Benson first proposed the project, there had been a huge uproar among town purists, including Tj, who didn't want to see the little mom-and-pop shops that made the town what it was replaced by a modern structure that stuck out like a sore thumb.

Tj entered the lobby through the glass door. Expecting to see the receptionist behind the desk, Tj was surprised to see Glen sitting in her office chair.

"Tj, what can I do for you?"

"I understand you managed Zachary Collins's estate."

"Yes, that's right. Did he tell you that?"

"He mentioned it." Tj thought it best not to bring Melanie into it. "I'm planning on speaking to Pastor Dan about the funeral and wondered if Zachary left a will with final wishes or instructions."

"Mr. Collins has a will on file," Glen confirmed. "It's quite simple. No final requests to speak of. Zachary was never interested in the financial aspect of his life and didn't want anyone to be burdened with it after his death, so he left instructions that whatever amount was left in his trust should be distributed to reputable charities as I saw fit."

"What about the house?" Tj asked.

Glen paused. "Zachary made arrangements to sell the house and the land it sits on to Lloyd Benson before he died. I'm surprised he didn't tell you."

Tj frowned. "He sold the house? Why would he do that?"

"We didn't really talk about the why. He asked me to draw up a contract selling the house and the land it sits on to Lloyd, with the provision that he wouldn't take possession of the property until after Zachary's death."

"That doesn't make any sense. Lloyd wants to tear down the house and build condos."

Glen placed an open hand on Tj's shoulder. "I know Mr. Collins was your friend and it might be hard for you to understand why he did what he did, but Zachary was an old man in ill health. I think he wanted things wrapped up before he passed on. He didn't have anyone to whom he wanted to leave the property, so why not sell it to someone who really wanted it?"

"Thank you for your time." Tj got up from her chair and said her final good-bye, then returned to her car. Glen hadn't said anything that would cast suspicion on him. Zachary really didn't seem to care about money, but she never thought he'd sell the house. He'd once told her the only way Lloyd Benson would get that house was over his dead body. Was it possible that was exactly what had happened?

CHAPTER 11

After Tj returned to the resort she walked over to the Grill to leave the gift voucher for Melanie before she forgot to do so. The rain that had been pounding the area all day finally stopped and the dark clouds that covered the sky began to part.

The Lakeside Bar and Grill was perched just behind the mile-long white sand beach for which Maggie's Hideaway was famous.

During the summer, guests of all ages played football and tossed Frisbees on the wide strip of sand that separated the deck of the Grill from the crystal-clear water of Paradise Lake. Today, however, the beach was deserted. The large wooden tables with colorful umbrellas that dotted the deck in the warmer months had all been moved into storage in preparation for the snow which, everyone knew, was just around the corner.

Tj filled out the voucher, then waved to Maude, Millie, Abe, and Andy, who were sharing hot turkey sandwiches with creamy mashed potatoes near a lake-view table. They smiled in greeting and called her over.

"Enjoying our fine weather?" Tj teased. She noticed both sisters wore the necklaces she'd commented about the last time she'd seen them.

"Actually, yes." Millie's eyes twinkled with delight. "The

storm, coupled with your delightful cabin and wood fire, has provided a very cozy setting."

"Started a bridge tournament that lasted most of the day," Abe, a man of around seventy with white hair and a stick-thin frame, added. "My Millie's a bold player. Haven't had such a wonderful time in ages."

My Millie?

"We were just making plans with the boys to have room service bring wine and dessert to our cabin a bit later." Millie blushed, turning her face the color of her cherry-red turtleneck sweater.

"I'll let room service know," Tj promised. "And dessert is on the house. I noticed there was cheesecake from my friend Jenna's restaurant in the kitchen when I walked through. She makes the best cheesecake around."

"Oh, I love cheesecake." Maude beamed. "Especially with a hearty cabernet."

"I noticed that you both have on the necklaces you were given by your father's church. I found the one my friend had." Tj pulled the necklace she'd been wearing around her neck since she'd retrieved it from Zachary's house out from under her sweater. "It looks like they match exactly."

"Yes, you are correct. This is a fidelity necklace given to female members of our group," Maude confirmed as she took a closer look.

"And you have no idea how my friend Zachary might have ended up with it?"

"Our group did tend to travel from time to time spreading the word," Millie informed me. "My papa was a talented speaker and the prayer meetings that were held in the towns we visited were quite spectacular. The group didn't travel as much after Maude and I got older but we did hear stories of meetings that attracted people from miles around. I suppose it is possible that your Zachary could have met one of the women in our group during one of these meetings."

"Do you think she would have given him the necklace?"

"Well I can't say as I know what could have occurred," Millie answered. "But like we explained before, there were women who left the group from time to time. I suppose that it is entirely possible that your friend knew one of these women."

Tj talked to the foursome a bit longer, then wandered across the room to the four-top in the corner to say hi to book-lover Kyle and dog-lover Carmen, who had wandered in while they were talking.

"How's everything going?" Tj asked the pair.

"Great. Pull up a seat," Kyle invited. "Coffee?"

"No thanks. I just wanted to say hi. I was wondering how the crate was working out." Carmen had brought a five-week-old puppy she'd rescued with her to Serenity where she'd come for an interview regarding a grant she desperately needed in order to complete her degree.

"Perfect," Carmen replied. "And the stuffed doggy mommy with the real heartbeat you included has been a godsend. Newton curls up with it and goes right to sleep after he's had his bottle of puppy formula."

"He's really a cutie. I love Echo, but even though I got him when he was only three months old, he already weighed over twenty pounds. I missed out on the fall-asleep-in-your-lap phase."

"You could always get another puppy," Carmen suggested. "My Grandma Bell used to love kittens, so every time her youngest cat got past the playful age, she'd just get another. She ended up with eleven cats by the time she passed away a few years ago."

"Eleven sounds like a bit much, but sometimes I think about it, although the house is bursting at the seams already. Besides, cute as they are, puppies take a lot of time, something I don't really have in abundance right now."

"Tell me about it," Carmen agreed. "I'm really enjoying Newton, but with my schedule at the university I worry about having enough time for him. If I get this grant, things are going to get even busier."

"I was going to ask you how your interview went."

"I haven't had it yet. The donor was supposed to contact me after I arrived, but I haven't heard a thing."

"Probably the storm," Tj surmised. "How about your job interview?" she asked Kyle.

"The same, I'm afraid."

"I guess it's lucky we were stuck here at the same time." Carmen smiled at Kyle. "At least we're keeping each other company."

"Yeah, lucky." Almost too lucky. "What did you say the name of your potential donor was?" she asked Carmen.

"Actually, I'm not really sure. Apparently the donor wanted to remain anonymous. I think it's a business or a group rather than a person. When my dissertation adviser told me about the potential donor she said *they* wanted to interview me before making a final decision. I guess the whole thing's a little unconventional, but I figured even if the grant didn't work out, the entire week was paid for, so what did I have to lose?"

Tj frowned. Kyle had a job interview with a company she'd never heard of and Carmen had an interview with an anonymous donor. Both had been given prepaid trips to the resort, and both trips were for the same ten-day period. Tj had no idea what was going on, but if she had to bet on it, she'd say the presence of these two was much more than coincidence.

Tj took the long way back to the house to clear her mind before the mayhem of making dinner and doing homework took over her evening. The clouds had taken on a bright red glow as the sun set behind the distant mountain. Damp earth mingled with the scent of pine and wood rose. Trout Creek, a seasonal tributary from the mountain peaks into the icy lake, had surpassed its boundaries, spilling its excess into the meadow beyond. Though closed for the season, the campground and stables had a tendency to flood during heavy runoff. Tj changed direction and headed toward the barn across the highway from the rest of the resort.

As she neared the large wooden building she noticed local veterinarian Rosalie Tyler's truck out front. Shasta, one of the resort's larger mares, was due to foal any day and Rosalie had been keeping a close eye on her. Increasing her pace to a jog, Tj paused in front of the open door. Her father stood with his back to her. Mike wasn't what you'd call handsome in a conventional way. He was tall, although not as tall as her grandfather, with broad shoulders and a slightly thickening waistline. His brown hair was peppered with gray and thinning on the top. Dark lashes framing his blue eyes had faded over the years, but the sparkle of merriment that accompanied each of his warm, inviting smiles was as bright and childlike as ever.

Rosalie stood next to Mike at the edge of the stall on the end. Tj suspected Dr. Tyler's relationship with her dad was more than a friendship, even though both insisted it wasn't. Rosalie shifted so the two stood face-to-face. Mike lifted his hand and gently touched her cheek. As he leaned in closer, Tj thought he might kiss her, but she said something Tj couldn't hear and he laughed and lowered his hand to his side. He turned and looked toward the stall behind him, and for the first time Tj noticed a small figure lying on the straw beyond them. Mike turned and knelt down, speaking gently to the animal. Tj chose that moment to join them.

"Oh, hey, Tj." Rosalie turned to greet her.

"My God, what happened?" Rosalie had the worst black eye Tj had ever seen.

"I'm afraid I had a run-in with my friend here." Rosalie nodded toward a newborn calf lying on the straw, a cast on one leg. He was drinking from the bottle her dad was holding.

"He kicked you?"

"I'll say. I was on my way home Saturday night when I passed the grazing meadow the ranchers from the valley use during the summer months. Guess they were rounding up the livestock before the storm hit, but in all the confusion this little guy broke his leg and was left behind."

"Intentionally?"

"No, I don't think so. Poor little thing was mostly hidden by the tall grass. I might not have noticed him myself if it weren't for the coyotes. They were dancing around, yipping and howling, so I slowed down to take a look and saw the little guy lying on the ground. Luckily I'd just come from town, where I'd splurged and bought the sweetest-looking steaks you've ever seen. Huge, thick ones, the kind that melt in your mouth when grilled. I actually hesitated for a second, but the poor calf was crying and thrashing around and the coyotes were drooling as they glared at it, so I grabbed my bag out of the truck and tossed those steaks as hard as I could into the forest. Then I grabbed that baby best as I could, but he was thrashing around so much he got me right in the eye. But I managed to get him into the back of my truck and take off before the coyotes came back for dessert."

"That's so ironic. You fed the coyotes your beefsteaks in order to save a future beefsteak."

"I'll tell you what," Rosalie said, laughing along with her, "after sacrificing what amounted to two hundred dollars' worth of steak, getting a black eye, and spending half the night patching him up, this little calf is going to die of old age."

Tj smiled as the little guy slurped the remainder of his dinner. "When I saw your truck, I thought maybe Shasta had dropped her foals."

"Should be anytime. We should keep a close eye on her, but I think she'll do fine."

"I talked to security. He should be popping a head in every hour or so," her dad informed her. "They have instructions to call my cell if it looks like she's going into labor."

One of the advantages of living on a resort was the twenty-four-hour security guard who kept an eye on the cabins, campground, restaurant, general store, and other shops in the cozy village.

"I heard about your friend Zachary," Rosalie commented. "I'm so sorry. I know this must be hard for you."

"The whole thing has come as a bit of a shock," Tj admitted. "I know you're friends with Lloyd Benson. Have you heard anything about his new project?"

"He showed me photos of a condominium complex he wants to build but I understand he had some issues with access. The last I heard the project had been put on hold until he could locate a different site."

"According to Glen Keller, who, as it turns out, is administrator of Zachary's estate, Zachary agreed to sell Lloyd his house and the land it sits on."

Mike frowned. "That doesn't seem like Zachary. The man liked his privacy."

"Exactly. I have a feeling something fishy is going on."

"I know that Lloyd's projects aren't always popular with

some of the locals, but he's a good man and an honest businessman," Rosalie commented. "I really don't think that he would get involved in a project which wasn't above board. I mean, why would he? He's been very successful as a developer. Why risk what he's built over a lifetime on a single project?"

Tj supposed Rosalie had a point. It didn't make sense that Glen would lie about Zachery selling the house but it also didn't make sense that Zachary would sell it. Something wasn't adding up.

"I'll see you guys back at the house," Tj said.

After leaving the barn, Tj called Doc. Maybe he had additional information regarding Zachary's cause of death. She knew he was waiting for the tox screen but surely he'd had time to complete an autopsy.

"Hey Doc. Any updates?" Tj asked when the man answered his cell.

"Actually yes. I was just about to call you. It turns out that the official cause of death for Zachary Collins was an overdose of sedatives."

"I went to Zachary's house after you mentioned sedatives, and while I will admit that I didn't have time to do a complete search, I did search his bathroom and the only thing I found were aspirin, blood pressure medication, and antacids."

"I don't know what to tell you. The man had sedatives in his system when he died. And not just a little. A lot."

"Do you know what kind?"

"I'm not sure yet. I should have a detailed toxicology report back in a couple of days. I notified the sheriff, who changed the official cause of death to apparent suicide."

"Why would Zachary commit suicide?"

"That I don't know."

By the time Tj had completed her conversation with Doc,

Rosalie had left and her dad had returned to the house. It sounded like Ben was making dinner and by the smell of it, Tj guessed they were in for some of his mouth watering lasagna and garlic bread.

"Something on your mind?" Mike asked as he took off his work boots and set them next to the shoes Tj had discarded in the mudroom.

"Actually, yes. I just spoke to Doc and he informed me that Zachary had a large quantity of sedatives in his system. Enough to kill him. It appears he committed suicide."

"And you don't think he did?"

"No. Despite what Doc said, the Zachary I knew wasn't the type to do something like that."

Mike paused before commenting. A look of compassion was evident on his face. "Don't get me wrong, I barely knew the man, but from the outside he seems to be exactly the type to commit suicide: aged recluse in ill health with deep emotional scars and no family or worldly connections. Honestly, honey, he's almost textbook."

"I know that's how it looks from the outside," Tj admitted as she followed her father into the living room in her stocking-clad feet. "But there was more to Zachary than met the eye. For one thing, he wasn't crazy, like most people thought. Something happened to him a long time ago. Something life-altering, for which he felt deep remorse. I don't know the whole story, but I know he was involved in an auto accident in which a man died. I got the impression he considered his life of solitude to be penance for whatever occurred. Maybe on the surface that makes him even more of a candidate for taking his own life, but Zachary wanted to live. He wanted to make amends for his sins."

"Make amends how?" Mike asked as he tossed several logs on the fire.

Tj shrugged. "I think he felt his suffering served as some sort of restitution. The thing is..." Tj hesitated. "When I saw him last week, he seemed—" Tj searched for the right word "—happy. As if a great burden had been lifted from his shoulders."

Mike took Tj's hand and gave it a reassuring squeeze. "You know how that sounds."

She looked her dad in the eye as a single tear slid down her cheek. "I realize Zachary was an old man in both mental and physical pain, and I can understand how he might have come to that decision." Tj took a deep breath as her emotions bubbled to the surface. "But my gut is telling me that Zachary would not kill himself."

"Maybe you're right. You've always had good instincts. Do you remember when you were six or seven and you befriended that old man who used to hang out in the campground?"

"Mr. Marbles." Mr. Marbles wasn't his real name, but everyone used to say the man's problem was that he was a few marbles short of a set, so Tj, who had taken the comment literally, gave him the bag of marbles she'd been collecting. Everyone started calling him Mr. Marbles from that point on.

"That's right, Mr. Marbles. Anyway, we had a rash of thefts in the cabins that started at about the same time Mr. Marbles showed up and everyone was convinced he was responsible, even though we had no proof. He was an obvious suspect. But you insisted that, even though Mr. Marbles sometimes asked the campers for a handout and wasn't beyond pilfering a half-eaten sandwich on a picnic table, he would never steal money or jewelry from our guests."

"And no one believed me," Tj remembered.

"Not even me," Mike admitted. "But in the end it turned out you were right. The culprit was one of our own employees who tried to frame Mr. Marbles by stashing a diamond necklace in his knapsack. Luckily there was a witness who saw what happened, and we arrested the right man. My point is, sometimes you have to believe what you know in your heart to be true, no matter what the evidence points to."

Tj thought about what her dad was telling her. He was right. She knew Zachary wouldn't kill himself. Something had happened on Friday night. Something unexplainable. She didn't know what it was, but she knew it was up to her to find out the truth. At this point it seemed that she was the only one even trying to prove that Zachary had met with foul play.

CHAPTER 12

Tuesday, October 26

Tj stood on the fifty-yard line of the high school football field, watching as the girls on her soccer team did their morning laps. The key to a successful soccer season was having a team whose fitness and endurance could outlast even their most skilled competitors.

"Carla, you're running like you have cement blocks stuck to your feet," Tj yelled through a megaphone. "Pick up the pace. And Lucy, you'd get a lot farther if you stopped flailing your arms like a chicken."

"Tj." A familiar voice sounded behind her.

Tj turned and greeted Kyle, her handsome guest. "What brings you out so early in the morning?"

"I heard there was a flea market in the town square and decided to start the hunt for the obligatory souvenirs for my family. I parked in the school parking lot and was on my way back to my car when I saw you standing here."

"It looks like you were successful." Tj nodded toward the armload of bags he carried.

"Yeah, too successful. The whole thing started off with a gift for my mom and escalated from there."

Tj laughed as Kyle set his packages on the grass. "Been there. Brittany, you're lagging this morning," Tj yelled. "Kick it up a notch. You're never going to make starting forward if you don't build up some endurance."

"Sorry." She turned back to Kyle. "The girls think they can take advantage of the fact that I'm distracted."

"If you need to get back…"

"No, I'm good. They know by now that I know when they're slacking off whether I'm looking at them or not. What did you get? For your mother, that is."

Kyle reached into a bag and pulled out a beautiful hand-sewn quilt. "The moment I saw this I knew she'd love it. It was ridiculously expensive, but I couldn't miss seeing the look on her face when I give it to her."

The quilt was made up of pieces of fabric in various shapes, sizes, colors, and patterns, puzzled together in such a way as to create the picture of two women sharing a picnic on a grassy knoll near a lake. "It's beautiful. It almost looks like someone painted the picture onto the fabric, rather than creating it from bits and pieces of other material."

"I know," Kyle agreed. "It reminded me of a picnic I went on with my parents when I was a kid. After my dad died a couple of years ago, my mom got out all the old photo albums and we went through them page by page, reminiscing about the good times we had. When I saw the quilt at the flea market the photo of that special day popped into my head."

"You're a really nice son."

"My mom, well, she's really special. She's had a hard couple of years. I know this sounds sappy, but I'd do anything to make her smile the way she did before my dad's heart attack."

"Finish the lap you're on, then take ten," Tj said, her megaphone lifted to her mouth once more. "Grab your gear and meet back here, ready to scrimmage. And Carla—" she turned toward a dark-haired girl walking toward the bleachers where a group of high school boys were hanging out "—lose the earrings."

The girl sighed but turned toward the locker room.

"Maybe I should get something like this for my room." Tj turned back toward Kyle, continuing their conversation without losing a beat.

"You live at the resort?" Kyle asked.

"Yeah. My mom died three months ago. The court granted me custody of my two half-sisters. I was living in town at the time, but I thought it best to move back home with my dad and grandpa, who have been fantastic about helping out."

"Wow. It must have been a tough transition."

"It has been, but we're all dealing. We've actually settled into a comfortable routine, and while I realize the situation is temporary, it's working for us at the moment. Did you have any other great finds?"

"I can show you later if you need to get back," Kyle offered.

"Nah. The girls usually have a way of stretching their ten into fifteen."

Kyle shrugged. "I bought a bunch of used paperbacks for myself and a hand-knitted scarf for my Aunt Susan." Kyle opened the bag to pull out the scarf. "I found some really cool sports memorabilia for my Uncle Pete, but I already dropped that off in the car. I bet you'd love the autographed photo I found of the Forty-Niners the year they beat the Denver Broncos in the Super Bowl in New Orleans."

"You're right." Tj smiled. "I'd love to see it." Tj looked at her watch. "Where are you parked?"

"Blue Honda over there." Kyle pointed to a compact near the southern fence.

"I have a few minutes. I'll walk you to your car."

Tj carried the bag with the quilt and Kyle carried the other bags as they walked toward his car. When Kyle opened the trunk to put the bags inside, Tj gasped.

"That bottle. Where did you get it?" she asked.

Kyle looked in the trunk. "This bottle?" Kyle picked it up. It was exactly like the one in Zachary's house. Other than the fact that it was now empty, Tj was sure it was the same bottle.

"Lady at the flea market. Said she'd just bought it over the weekend and I was lucky to happen to come by when I did. It's from the 1918 centennial bottling of McClelland's Scotch. My grandpa collects old bottles and he loves scotch." Kyle seemed oblivious to the pallor that had fallen over Tj's face. "It's the perfect gift."

It was possible the bottle Kyle bought was not the same one she'd seen in Zachary's house, but given that it was almost a hundred years old, she doubted it.

"Are you okay? You look a little ill."

She took a deep breath. Should she tell him about the scotch? Kyle seemed like a nice guy, but she didn't really know him. Could Kyle have drugged Zachary and then taken the bottle?

Tj looked toward the field. "I should get back to the girls. Looks like they kept the ten to ten today. I'll have to stop by and see the photo later."

"Sure, anytime. I have some other stuff you might enjoy seeing too."

"By the way—" Tj turned back toward Kyle after she had taken a few steps "—what did you say the name of the woman who sold you the bottle was?"

"I didn't. Actually, I don't know. She never said and I didn't think to ask."

"Can you describe her?"

"She was between fifty-five and sixty, short blond hair that curled on the ends, maybe five foot six. I'm sure one of the regulars can tell you, if you're really interested."

Tj tried to look nonchalant. "It's no big deal. I have a friend who collects glass. I thought he might be interested." Tj waved one final time and then headed toward the center of the field, where her team was gathering.

She was certain the bottle Kyle had was Zachary's. Zachary had died on Friday. Kyle said the woman indicated she'd just bought the bottle over the weekend. Someone must have drugged Zachary and then taken it. It seemed odd that someone would commit a murder, steal a bottle of scotch from the scene, and then turn around and sell the bottle, creating a trail right back to him. A bottle from the 1918 centennial bottling of McClelland's Scotch was pretty distinctive and not easy to come by. Still, Tj couldn't come up with a better theory as to how the bottle had gotten from Zachary's house to Kyle's trunk. Since Kyle didn't even know Zachary, and he was carrying around the missing bottle in his truck, it seemed unlikely he was involved in Zachary's death. Still, it wouldn't hurt to take a closer look at the guy, so Tj called Dylan and shared with him her suspicion regarding the missing bottle.

Right after practice Tj needed to grab a quick lunch, then prepare for her first choir class. She'd have to wait until school was out before she could head over to The Antiquery and ask Helen if she knew who might have sold Kyle the bottle. Helen knew everyone, especially those who dealt in antiques.

*   *   *

Tj wasn't expecting much, but when she walked into room A5 and found that her choir consisted of a half dozen misfits, she knew she was in trouble.

Greg had made it perfectly clear it was her duty not only to supervise the group but to mold and hone them into a functioning body that could perform in a public setting. Given that she had absolutely zero musical background, she had hoped Greg was wrong in his assessment of the recruits his wife had managed to come up with on such short notice, and this magical choir was already groomed and ready to perform.

"Good afternoon, everyone," Tj began. "Most of you know me from physical education, but given that we are assembled here to form a choir, I thought we could go around the room and introduce ourselves. I'll start. My name is Coach Jensen, and I am excited to have the opportunity to take on the role of staff adviser for this very special group."

"I heard we were the last choice and you got stuck with us." Ryder Finnegan, a socially aggressive boy who was more often in detention than not, chimed in. Everyone in town knew his father was a drunk who hadn't had a job in more than four years, so most folks tended to give the young man a break in spite of his difficult personality.

"You know what they say about leaving the best for last," Tj said. "Since you seem eager to share, why don't you start us off by telling us your name and why you decided to join choir?"

"You know my name." His blue eyes flashed with annoyance.

"I do, but others in the room may not."

"Name is Ryder." His long blond bangs draped over one eye as he glared at her with the other. "I'm in this dumb group because Mr. Talbot told me he'd forgive the hundred and fifty hours of community service I racked up over the summer if I joined the choir."

Jim Talbot was a probation officer in charge of community service for underage minor crimes, like petty theft, possession, and truancy.

"Okay, I can work with that. How about you?" Tj nodded to a large-boned girl she didn't remember seeing in any of her PE classes.

"Rhonda. I don't like getting sweaty, and Mr. Remington said I could skip PE for the rest of the year if I joined the choir."

"I see." Tj wasn't a fan of letting kids who most needed an hour of exercise avoid the only class in which they were likely to get it. "There are a lot of fun options to the traditional calisthenics many people think of when they hear the word PE. Have you thought of trying soccer or dance?"

"Don't like to run and don't like to dance."

"You have to dance," Marley Davis spoke up. "The student council voted to make this a show choir, like in that TV show."

Rhonda snorted. Marley was the president of the student council and, Tj suspected, the only member of the group who gave a flying leap whether the choir was a regular or a show one. The girl had gumption, she'd give her that, but it was going to be close to impossible to turn six misfits, none of whom appeared to have any actual musical talent, into a regular choir that could serenade the old folks at the senior center, let alone a show choir that had to sing and dance at competitions.

"Okay, since Marley brought it up, let's talk direction. Marley has suggested a show choir, but I'm thinking it might be easier to just focus on being a regular choir."

"Mr. Remington said we could be a show choir," Marley argued. "The student council voted on it. I already have my solo picked out for our first competition but we're going to need more students."

"Maybe we can hand out fliers and hold tryouts," one of the students suggested.

"Good idea. I'll make up some fliers, you all can try to recruit friends and classmates. Normally our group will meet Tuesdays and Thursdays, but due to the Pumpkin Festival we'll skip this Thursday and meet back here a week from today."

CHAPTER 13

After school, Tj dropped her sisters off at a friend's, agreeing to pick them up in a couple of hours, then headed through the festive little town toward The Antiquery. Serenity, originally founded to support a large lumber operation, now boasted a charming downtown district. It consisted of a single main street lined on one side by Paradise Lake and on the other by a myriad of cozy shops displaying their wares in artfully decorated windows. The downtown strip was bordered to the north by a narrow stone bridge built more than seventy years earlier to allow a dry crossing of the Paradise River, and to the south by a recently developed community park where summer concerts and local events like the annual pumpkin carving competition were held.

Like all the other storefronts on Main Street, The Antiquery was dressed out in fall colors. Helen had spent the last couple of weeks working on a display from the 1950s centered on the antique jukebox, old-fashioned soda machine, and red vinyl booths she'd found in someone's garage. Helen was meticulous in her mission to buy the highest-quality antiques, then painstakingly restore them to their original magnificence. Each piece was grouped as part of a period exhibit, where scrupulous attention to detail provided for museum-quality displays.

"Something smells good," Tj commented as she walked

through the kitchen door from the alley which ran behind the shops on Main Street.

"I'm experimenting with a new recipe for the cookie exchange," Jenna said.

"The cookie exchange as in the Christmas cookie exchange, which is like six weeks away?"

"I know it seems ridiculous, but I have a reputation for being the best cook in town—a reputation, I might remind you, that keeps this restaurant in the black—so it's important that I bring something both fantastic and unique. The closer we get to the actual event, the more hectic things will get around here, so I usually try to experiment with a few ideas whenever I get the chance."

"What are you working on?"

"It's a secret. You'll just have to wait six weeks to find out. How about you? Any secret recipes you're playing around with?"

"Thought I might add butterscotch chips to the Nestlé Toll House cookies I usually make. Does that count as a secret recipe?"

"Actually, for you it does."

Tj hated to cook and wasn't ashamed to admit it. Maybe she brought the same chocolate chip cookies every year, but even Jenna had to admit they were the best chocolate chip cookies around. She'd leave spending hours in the kitchen, baking batch after batch of some innovative idea, up to her domestically talented best friend.

"Here to mooch a late lunch?" Jenna asked.

"No, but I'll have a cookie."

"I have three batches that I baked earlier in the day. Take one of those. My new recipe isn't quite ready to be tasted yet."

Tj grabbed two cookies from the rack. "Are these the same ones you made for the field trip?" Tj referred to the third grade field trip she'd chaperoned for Ashley's class the previous week.

"They are. I totally forgot to ask you how it went."

"It was fun," Tj hedged. "If you classify a hot and stuffy bus ride lasting an hour and a half in each direction with twenty-three eight-year-olds, most of whom either had to pee or puke at least once, as fun. The children's museum was cool, though. Tons of interactive stuff to play with. And Ashley seemed to have a good time, which made any discomfort I had to endure totally worth it."

"She doing any better?" Jenna wondered.

"Honestly," Tj said, "I'm not sure. She did really well on the field trip. She seemed to enjoy herself and got along well with the other kids. But let's not forget the whole reason I got a sub for my classes in the first place was because Ashley has been so disruptive since she started school in September that her teacher wasn't going to let her attend if I didn't go along to keep an eye on things."

"It's only been three months since her mom died," Jenna reminded her. "You're doing your best, given the circumstances. These things take time."

"Well, her teacher doesn't think my best is good enough. And it's not like I really blame her. A single disruptive student can bring the whole group down. Gracie tends to express her pain through periods of uncontrollable sobbing, but Ashley prefers to work out her sorrow with her fists."

"Sounds like her big sister." Jenna grinned, light blue eyes dancing with delight. "I remember you being the cause of a few black eyes in preschool after your mom left. In fact, I'm fairly certain I was the recipient of one of your larger masterpieces."

Tj couldn't help but smile. "I have to say that black eye was one of my favorites." Not only had Tj decorated Jenna's face when she tried to steal her red crayon but, Jenna being Jenna even then, had decided the best way to avoid a repeat episode was to befriend the unhappy little girl. They'd been best friends ever since.

"Thing is," Tj sighed, "I was mad and acted out for a few weeks, but then I got over it."

"Actually, I'm pretty sure your tendency to solve your problems with your fists lasted more than a few weeks. Things got better after your dad signed you up for that martial arts class. Maybe something like that would work for Ashley."

"You could be right. Maybe I'll look into it. Right now I need to ask your mom a question. She in the front?"

"Should be."

Tj walked through the dining area of the café to the antique side and found Helen working on her newest display.

"Nice touch." Tj admired the old magazines from the nineteen fifties stacked on a table near the old-fashioned soda fountain.

"Thanks. I think the display is coming along quite nicely. I've had folks dropping by all week to give me their input on the subject. I picked up a twelve-piece set of antique cola glasses at the flea market this weekend."

"Speaking of that: there was a woman about fifty-five selling glass and other used items at the flea market this weekend."

"Short blond hair?" Helen asked.

"Yeah, you know her name?"

"Connie Beckett. She just recently moved to the area. Runs a little shop out of her garage."

"You know where she lives?"

"Corner of Pine and Fourth. Why, are you in the market for something specific?"

"No, I just heard she had nice pieces. Thought I'd check it

out. You wouldn't happen to have her phone number, would you?"

"I don't, but I suppose you could just go by her place."

"Yeah, I might do that. Thanks."

"Before you leave, I wanted to ask you about the Halloween Ball."

"What about it?" Tj asked.

"Dotty Harris told me you turned down her offer to fix you up with her son for the ball. I really think you should reconsider. Between you and me, David's a real catch compared to most of the eligible men in this town."

Tj loved Helen. She really did. After Tj's own mother left town, Helen had stepped in to ensure she wouldn't suffer from the lack of a woman's touch. She'd treated Tj like one of her own daughters, but, unfortunately, part of Helen's mothering package included constant interference in all parts of her daughters' lives.

"I appreciate you trying to look out for me," Tj began diplomatically, "and you know I value your opinion, but I'd really rather find a date for the ball on my own. I hope you understand."

"Of course, dear. I have to remember that you're growing up."

Growing up? I'm twenty-six.

"I'm sure a smart and pretty girl like you will have many men to choose from. Although," Helen paused, "the very least I can do is help you with your costume. We'll turn you into a princess. I promise that when I'm done with you, the men in this town will be left speechless."

Tj had a feeling she was going to regret agreeing to Helen's plan, but she couldn't deny she was curious to see what Helen had in mind. Besides, one of her secret fantasies had been to have her mom help her dress for the prom or some other special night, a secret wish she knew would never be granted by her own mother.

"Please?" Helen persuaded.

"Well, okay. I guess. But nothing pink."

"Trust me. You'll be the belle of the ball."

After Tj left The Antiquery she headed toward Fourth and Pine. The neighborhood where Connie lived was laid out with numbered streets running east and west and streets with tree names running north and south. Tj parked on the street in front of the two story structure. Since she had never met the woman who sold Kyle the bottle, she decided to act as a prospective customer.

"Can I help you?" The woman asked after Tj rang the bell.

"Hi, my name is Tj. Sorry to bother you at home but I was hoping that you could help me with a gift for my grandfather. I understand that you sell vintage glass."

The woman indicated that Tj should come in. "I sell a lot of different things. Did you have something specific in mind?"

"Actually yes. My friend Kyle bought a bottle from you this weekend. It was from the 1918 centennial bottling of McClelland's Scotch. I'd love to have a bottle just like it and was wondering where you got it."

"I bought it from Dumpster Doug."

Tj knew that Dumpster Doug was a pack rat who went through the dumpsters around town looking for objects to sell.

"Did Doug say where he got it?"

"I'm sorry, I didn't ask. I never do. Doug brings me a lot of items to sell, most of which are worthless, but every now and then he comes up with something good. If you are interested in that specific bottle I'm sure I can track one down for you if you give me some time."

"Thanks, but I don't want you to go to all that effort."

"Would you like to take a look at what I do have in stock?"

"Sure," Tj replied as the woman turned toward the garage. It would be rude not to buy anything.

After Tj loaded the bag full of used books that she'd purchased into her car, she headed toward the alley behind Main Street to see if Doug happened to be scavenging that afternoon. Unfortunately he wasn't, so Tj headed across town to pick up her sisters.

CHAPTER 14

"Tj," Ashley said as she buckled Gracie into her car seat.

"Yes, honey?"

"Do you think we can get some paint for my room?"

Tj held her breath as her heart skipped a beat. "Sure, honey. I think Chase Hardware is still open. We can get it now, if you want."

"Okay," Ashley agreed as she buckled her seat belt.

Tj forced herself not to shout for joy as she pulled slowly onto Main Street. After the accident, she'd decided to have the badly damaged body of her mom cremated, which Tj later realized had been a huge mistake, her first of many. When she broke it to the girls that their mom had passed, Gracie had been sad but accepting, but Ashley had steadfastly refused to believe her mother was never coming home. She was certain there'd been some huge mistake, and it had been someone else's mom who had died.

When Tj brought the girls to the resort to live, she'd wanted to redecorate the male-dominated guestrooms right away. Gracie had been more than willing to let Tj replace the dark wood paneling in her room with light colors and stuffed animals in a Noah's Ark theme, but Ashley had insisted there was no reason to redecorate her room since her mom was coming to get her any day. Tj had tried many times over the first few weeks to get Ashley to allow her to redecorate, but eventually she'd taken her dad's counsel to let her come around to it in her own time.

"What did you have in mind?" Tj asked as she pulled into the parking lot of the family-operated store.

"Well," Ashley began, "Kristi has pink and white in her room and I really like it, but then I thought I'd do something a little more unik."

"You mean unique?"

"Yeah. I want something different. I like the green wall. I guess we could replace all that wood and hunting stuff with something that has purple in it."

"Purple and green. I like it."

Tj helped the girls out of the car before grabbing a red shopping cart and entering the store through the double-wide doors. "Dylan," she said as she almost ran into the man leaving the store with his own cart.

"Tj. What brings you here?"

"These are my sisters, Ashley and Gracie. This is Deputy Caine," Tj said, introducing the girls. "We're here to buy paint and wallpaper for Ashley's room."

"You painting your room too?" Gracie asked, noticing that his basket was full of paint cans and paintbrushes.

"Actually, a whole house. I just bought the Montgomery place," he explained to Tj.

"Really? That place is huge. And a total wreck," she added. "But huge. It must have ten bedrooms. I think you're going to need more paint."

"I know the place needs a little work," Dylan said.

Tj raised an eyebrow.

"Okay, a lot of work. But the location can't be beat. A huge piece of property right on the lakeshore with plenty of room for Kiva to run to her heart's content."

"Kiva?"

"My Husky. I'm afraid the old girl is getting tired of hotel living. Not only did Mr. Montgomery give me a killer deal on the property, but he's going to let us move in right away."

"You have any kids?" Gracie asked.

"No, it's just me and Kiva."

"Oh." Gracie sighed.

"You sound disappointed."

"Me and Ashley are the two newest kids in school. If you had kids, we wouldn't be the newest anymore."

Tj noticed that Dylan tried to hide his smile as the girl pouted over her misfortune.

"Can you keep a secret?" he asked her.

"Sure." Gracie leaned in close as Dylan knelt down to her height.

"I was just at the video store on Fifth Street buying a game for my nephew Justin's birthday. The woman who helped me told me the owners were retiring and the new family who bought the place will be moving in next month. I heard they have three kids around your age."

"I'm five and Ashley is eight," Gracie volunteered.

"Seems about right."

Gracie's face lit up like a hundred-watt bulb.

It was common knowledge the Connelly's had sold the store and were moving, but it was sweet the way Dylan made Gracie feel special by sharing a secret with her.

"So what color are you going to paint your room?" Dylan turned his attention to Ashley.

"Purple and green."

"Purple and green; bold. I like it. Are you thinking curtains or blinds? Because personally, I'm torn."

"Both," Ashley decided. "Blinds to keep the sun out and

curtains for decoration. Maybe those short ones that drape around the window."

"Swag," Tj supplied.

"Yeah, those."

"You seem to have an eye for design," Dylan complimented her. "Maybe I should have you out to the house to give me some suggestions once I get the heavy work done."

"'Kay." Ashley tried to seem nonchalant, but Tj could tell she was about to burst at the seams with pride that the handsome deputy wanted her opinion.

In the three minutes they'd been in the store, Dylan had managed to charm her sisters. They both seemed a little in love with him now. Heck, she was a little in love with him herself. Handsome, good job, dog lover, liked kids...

"I wanted to talk to you more about the matter we discussed yesterday." Tj was purposely vague in front of the girls. "Will you be in your office tomorrow?"

Dylan took out his phone and consulted his calendar. "Can you come by around four?"

"That should work fine."

"Okay, I'll see you then." Dylan waved as he walked toward the front door.

"Okay, where should we start?" Tj turned to Ashley as Dylan left the store.

"Wallpaper," Ashley decided.

"I think the books are in the back, near the contractor's counter." Tj turned and headed down a narrow aisle.

"We'll have to order it?" Ashley was clearly disappointed.

"Probably," Tj said. "Although, Mr. Chase usually keeps a few prints in stock. Maybe we'll luck out and he'll have something you like."

"Evening, Tj. Girls. What can I help you with?"

"Wallpaper," Ashley answered.

"I can order you anything in any of those books." He nodded toward the table. "And I have these prints in stock." He handed Tj a binder with samples.

"How long will it take to get the paper if we order it?" Tj asked after handing the sample binder to Ashley.

"It depends on the manufacturer. I've got a list here somewhere." Mr. Chase had started rummaging around in a drawer when the phone rang.

Tj waited while the man answered the call. The store hadn't changed a bit since she used to come in as a child. Faded gray linoleum covered the floor. An old coffeepot sat half empty on the long pine counter that extended the full length of the back wall. Narrow aisles were packed with as much inventory as the little store could hold.

"You know I want to bid the project," Tj heard him say, "but we both know I don't have the kind of capital it'd take to front the inventory. I'd need a substantial deposit for a job of that size." Tj watched as Mr. Chase frantically took notes on a dirty yellow legal pad. "I realize the bigger stores off the mountain wouldn't need such a big deposit, but you know I'll give you better service than you'll get from one of those warehouses," the man responded. "Yeah, I can be there. Just let me know when."

Tj wandered over to look at paint samples while Mr. Chase finished his conversation.

"Sorry about that," the man said as he walked up behind her a few minutes later. "Kurt Brown got the contract to build those condos Lloyd Benson is developing down by the lake. He's soliciting bids for suppliers and subcontractors."

"Already?" Tj asked. "The council hasn't even voted on it yet."

"Kurt said it's all but a done deal. Lucky thing too. Before this job came along, Kurt was talking bankruptcy. Took a bath on that project he built last year up at Angel Mountain. Guess he wants to hit the ground running once the council votes so he can pay off the loan he had to take against his house. Be a shame to lose the place. It's a real beaut."

Tj frowned. "Did Kurt say when Lloyd hired him?"

"Didn't say, but I gathered it was at least a few weeks ago. Sounded like he'd already done quite a bit of ground work. Mentioned he almost lost the project after putting in a good deal of time and his own money working up a bid. He seemed real happy the project was back on track."

"Did he mention why he almost lost the project?"

"I'm not sure but I guess Lloyd got whatever problem they were having all cleared up. About the paint—I'm running a special on the store brand. I can mix you up any color you want."

After spending over an hour in the hardware store, Ashley finally settled on light lavender paint and wallpaper with small flowers in a darker shade of purple and dark green leaves on a cream-colored background that Mr. Chase had in stock. The dark brown carpeting in the room was definitely going to have to go, so Tj ordered burgers to be brought over from the Grill while the entire family got to work moving furniture, pulling up old carpet, and stripping walls.

In any other circumstance Tj might have waited until the weekend to begin the project, but after weeks of hoping the fragile little girl would accept the changes in her life and begin to rebuild, Tj didn't want to give her the opportunity to change her mind. Her dad had been right when he'd counseled her to let Ashley set the pace of her grieving process. Just a few short weeks ago Ashley wouldn't have welcomed the fresh paint and new carpet, but as they worked side by side, debating the merits of bunk beds versus full, Tj felt for the first time that Ashley had finally come home.

It was past nine o'clock before Tj decided they'd best call it a night. Ben retired to the den to watch an old movie while Mike went to check on Shasta. Tj supervised showers and got the girls off to bed in Gracie's room. After everyone was settled, Tj made some herbal tea and settled into the living room with Echo and Cuervo.

The phone call she'd overheard between Mr. Chase and Kurt Brown had been bugging her all night. It sounded like Lloyd Benson wasn't the only one who had something to gain by Zachary's death. If Kurt was as hard up for money as Mr. Chase indicated and the project that would bail him out was threatened, could he have drugged Zachary to get the project back on track? Of course if Zachary actually had already sold the house to Lloyd, killing Zachary to force a sale wouldn't be necessary. Still, she figured she'd mention Kurt and his involvement in Lloyd's project when she met with Dylan the next day.

She thought of the handsome deputy. He'd been so good with the girls. He wasn't really her type, or at least she was working hard to convince herself that he wasn't. Her life was complicated enough without adding an unobtainable crush to the mix, but she couldn't help but think about the dimple in the corner of his mouth and the way his eyes crinkled when he smiled.

She should be exhausted from a long, emotional day, but instead felt oddly energized. She'd been thinking a lot about

Zachary and wishing she'd tried harder to know him. For years she spent several hours every week with him, but she never truly learned about his life or his past. It was especially odd, Tj realized, for someone with her natural tendency to get involved in the intimate details of *everyone's* lives. Maybe in the end he'd wanted to reach out to her, but she'd been so involved in her own life that she'd never given him the chance.

Tj had all but decided to head up to bed when her dad called to tell her that Shasta was in labor. Looked like it was going to be a late night after all.

CHAPTER 15

Wednesday, October 27

"Hey, Coach, you wanted to see me?" Brittany Baxter popped her head into Tj's office the next morning.

"Come on in and have a seat." Tj yawned.

Brittany hesitated. Every available surface, including the chair in front of the desk, was piled high with file folders.

"Sorry." Tj got up from behind the desk and cleared the chair, setting the files on top of the cabinet. "I've been working on the grant for the new gym and the paperwork has been a lot more demanding than I'd anticipated. I asked you to stop by to see how things are going," Tj said. "At home, that is."

Brittany, a senior and the captain of the ski team, had a good chance of getting a full-ride scholarship to the college of her choice with another winning season. There was even talk that she had a shot at the national team, possibly even the Olympics. It would be a shame if this thing with her parents messed it up for her.

Brittany shrugged. "They're goin'. Guess you could even say things are looking up, if you count a total refusal of my parents to speak to one another as better than constant yelling."

"That bad, huh?"

"Worse. They keep using me as a go-between. 'Brittany, tell your mother to pass the salt.' 'Brittany, tell your father to get it himself.' So over it."

"Your parents are both living in the house?"

"Crazy, huh? Both want the other to leave and neither is willing to budge. They fight over everything. At first I was really upset that my parents wanted me to leave while they worked through the divorce, but now I can't wait to split. There are days when I don't care if I ever see either of them again."

Tj leaned forward, crossing her arms over the small space she'd cleared on her desk. "I know it's hard, but I'm sure they both really care about you."

"As if." Brittany started to cry. "They barely remember I exist. This is my last year before college. I thought senior year would be the best year of my life, but instead it totally sucks. Mom won't let me go out with my friends, and she's been awful to my boyfriend. He won't even hang out anymore. I'll probably lose my college scholarship if I have to change schools, and my parents are spending so much money on expensive attorneys from off the mountain, trying to one-up one another, that they won't have any of my college fund left to foot the bill. It's not fair."

"No," Tj agreed, "it's not." She handed Brittany a tissue. "If there's anything I can do, just let me know."

"Thanks." Brittany blew her nose. "I think I'm going to crash with Jilli. Her mom said it was cool. I really need to focus, and there's no way I can do that with all the yelling. If I do well at nationals this year, I have a real shot at making the national team. It's weird, but just being around Jilli gives me perspective. You know what I mean?"

Tj did know. Jilli's dad had been killed in a skiing accident the winter before. No matter how much Brittany hated what her parents were doing and how much it was disrupting her life, at least they were still around to drive her crazy.

"Sorry to interrupt, Coach Jensen, but you have a visitor," the second period student office worker said, sticking her head in the door. "Your phone's off the hook or I would have buzzed you."

Tj glanced down at her desk to see a stack of paperwork had knocked the receiver off the phone cradle. The grant she was in charge of writing was kicking her butt more than she wanted to admit. "Do you know who it is?"

The girl shrugged. "Some old guy."

"Give me a couple minutes, then show him in."

Tj looked at her watch, then turned to Brittany. "I'll probably be a few minutes late to class. I planned to have the girls do a weight circuit today. The workout logs are on the top of that pile over there." Tj pointed to a pile near the door. "Go ahead and take them and have the girls start stretching. I should be there in a few."

After Brittany left Tj tried to straighten her desk to the point where she could actually see over the stacks of paper. Other than the small space directly in front of her, the entire surface was piled high with blueprints, community testimonials, and financial projections for the new gym.

"Tj Jensen?" A tall man with silver hair who looked to be in his sixties asked as he poked his head into the office.

"Come on in and have a seat." She motioned to the chair Brittany had recently vacated.

"My name is Trent Jackson." He smiled as he folded himself into the small chair. "I spoke to a woman by the name of Helen Henderson who works at The Antiquery who told me you were friends with Zachary Collins."

"Yes, we were friends. Did you know him?"

"No, I never met the man, but he used to be friends with my dad, Will Jackson, a long time ago."

"Your dad used to live here?"

"He lived here for a summer in 1953. Worked over at Steamers Wharf as a deck hand. He said he met a lot of good people during the short time he was here, including your friend, Zachary Collins. I was in the area and thought I might look him up. I was sorry to hear he passed away."

"Helen must've told you he died just a few days ago."

"She did. She said if anyone in the area knew anything about his personal life it would be you. I'm actually on my way to the Bay Area but figured it was worth a stop if you had time to talk."

"I have a class in a few minutes, but if you don't mind walking over to the weight room with me, we can talk while the girls work out. They know the drill, so all I really have to do is provide an adult presence."

"I'd like that."

Tj picked up a clipboard, then showed Trent into the hallway, locking her office door behind her. The wide hallway was lined with gray lockers stacked three high. Every twenty feet or so, a doorway led into the classrooms the physical education department used in the absence of a real gym. The weight room was three doors down from Tj's office. She indicated the folding chairs in the corner of the room where Trent could sit while she quickly took roll call, made a few announcements, and demonstrated the proper form for a new exercise she wanted the girls to try.

Once finished, Tj quickly did the math in her head as she sat down next to him. "So Zachary would have been around twenty-one when your dad knew him."

"I'm not really sure. My dad has a photo with four men including him in it. He was twenty-two at the time, and the men all look about the same age."

"Did you bring the photo?"

"No, I'm afraid I didn't think to."

"Any idea who the other two men are?" Zachary never talked about his life before she met him, and Tj found she was wildly curious about what kind of man he'd been before the accident. According to what she'd been able to find out through town gossip, he'd been quite the partier and ladies' man.

"The other two men were named Timothy Bell and Arthur Holland. Neither man is still alive, but from the stories my dad told, it sounded like they shared a wild summer. I was interested in learning more about my dad's time at the lake since he turned out to be a very conservative history professor. Somehow the stories he told and the man I knew never quite lined up."

Prudence Holland, a friend of the family, had a late husband named Arthur. Interesting how Prudence never mentioned that her husband and Zachary were friends. Even more so that Zachary never mentioned it, considering Arthur had lived in the same town as he did until the day he died. Something must have happened to drive a wedge between the men. Tj wished she'd tried harder to get Zachary to talk about his life before his self-imposed imprisonment. She guessed now she'd never know.

"Did your father stay in touch with the men after he left?" Tj wondered.

"For a while, but from what I could gather there was some type of falling out. Apparently all four men set their sights on the same woman. Once my dad realized he didn't have a shot he started dating my mom and more or less severed his relationship with the other three."

"Yet he kept the picture?"

"I know. I thought it was odd too. He claims he knew the men for less than a year and completely severed the relationship with them shortly after that, yet he kept a photo of them on his desk until the day he died. He talked a lot about his summer here—the parties they attended, the trouble they got into. He never really talked much about what happened after that."

"And you were hoping Zachary could fill in some of the blanks about what happened?" Tj guessed.

"More or less." Trent shrugged. "To be honest, I never really thought about it much until a man named John Henry called my mom a couple of months ago looking for my dad on Zachary Collins's behalf. He was actually trying to track down any descendants of Timothy Bell, and was hoping he kept in touch with the woman Timothy eventually married. He was unaware my dad had passed away. Since I was coming out west anyway, I thought I'd detour and see if I could talk to Mr. Collins. Wish I had gotten here a few days sooner."

"I'm not sure how receptive Zachary would have been to your questions. Something happened when he was a young man that turned him into a total recluse. Now that he has passed, I'm realizing there was so much I never knew about him."

Trent bowed his head. "It's surprising how many unanswered details of a loved one's life don't seem important until they're gone and all you have left are memories. You start thinking of all of the questions you'd never thought to ask but suddenly wish you had. I've been driving my mom crazy since my dad passed, asking her about all the seemingly unimportant details of her life, but I realize now that someday I'll wish I knew where she went to elementary school and who her first big crush was."

Tj thought about her grandfather who was getting on in

years. She knew a lot about the man, but there were also a lot of gaps. Things she'd never asked. Things he'd never shared. Maybe she'd make more of a point to sit down and talk to him.

Tj talked with Trent a while longer, then dismissed her class and walked him out to the parking lot. Her conversation with Trent had brought up some questions. If Zachary and Prudence's husband Arthur were friends in 1953 and Prudence married Arthur in 1954, was it possible Prudence knew Zachary? Prudence may have even been the woman the four men fought over. Trent said his father married another woman and Tj knew Zachary never married, so in all likelihood the winning suitor was either Timothy Bell or Arthur Holland. She knew Prudence usually had lunch with her best friend, Hazel Whipple, at the post office and decided she'd stop by during her prep period and ask a few questions.

CHAPTER 16

When Tj arrived at the post office at exactly 11:23, Hazel, who always wore a proper shin-length day dress and sturdy one-inch heels, was on a stepladder changing a light bulb. "Let me help you with that." Tj hurried over and steadied the ladder for the tall, thin, woman with short, roller-curled hair. "Climb down and I'll finish up for you."

"Nonsense. I've been changing light bulbs since before you were born," she said. "Since before your father was born even. I think I can handle it."

At seventy-one, Hazel was feistier than most women half her age. Technically she should have retired from the post office with a full pension years ago, but the spunky widow was determined to remain employed until they hauled her away in a body bag, a sentiment she often shared when concerned friends tried to talk her into slowing down. She'd never had children and her husband had died more than thirty years earlier. The post office, which had been a constant in her life for more than fifty years, seemed to be the only family Hazel had left.

"You here for your dad's package?" she asked after replacing the bulb and climbing down. Folding the stepladder, she carried it back to the storeroom before taking her place behind the old counter, which she'd decorated with fall accents as she did every year.

"My dad has a package?"

"New seal for the generator pump at the resort. He asked me to keep an eye out for it. I gather the old one is leaking like a sieve. They don't make stuff the way they used to. In my day, you could buy a piece of equipment and it would last a lifetime. It didn't cost a month's wages, either."

Tj realized she was in for one of the soapbox back-in-my-day speeches for which Hazel was famous. Over the years Tj had discovered it was best just to listen politely and nod at appropriate intervals.

"Folks these days seem to have lost all perspective on what things are worth," Hazel continued. "Why, that new coffee shop on the corner charges almost five dollars for one of its fancy cups of brew. Things used to cost what they were worth and not a penny more. I tell you, if the people in this country don't mend their ways we're headin' for another depression."

Tj doubted that, but she didn't say as much. "I know what you mean," she responded politely. "I'll take the seal as long as I'm here, but actually I was looking for Pru."

"Pru's in the ladies' room," Hazel said and she handed Tj the package from behind the counter.

"Not anymore." Prudence walked into the room. At eighty-three, she was what Tj thought of as a handsome woman. Tall and lean with angular features, a beaklike nose, and a head of short white hair, the woman commanded attention wherever she went. It wasn't surprising that Hazel and Pru were such close friends. If there was anyone in town who could match Hazel wit for wit, it was Pru and her outspoken manner. Pru had once told Tj that the best thing about being older than sin was that you could say anything you wanted, no matter how rude, and no one would think anything about it.

"Interesting choice." Prudence eyed her up and down.

"Huh?"

"The outfit you have on. Interesting choice."

Tj looked down at her black running shorts and extra-large Serenity High School sweatshirt. First Helen and now Pru? Was there a new fashion police in town?

"I just came from school." Tj explained. "And I have soccer practice later," she added for good measure. "It didn't seem worth it to change just to run a few errands."

"Uumph," Pru grunted. "Never gonna get a man that way."

Tj started to explain that she wasn't trying to get a man but decided to choose the path of least resistance and change the subject. She was unsure of how Prudence would respond to her inquiry, but anything had to be better than the subject they were on. "I was speaking to a visitor who stopped by the high school to inquire about Zachary. It seems his father knew Arthur," she began.

"My Arthur?"

"Apparently so. I guess they were friends a long time ago. His name was Will Jackson."

"Will's son is here?" Prudence actually looked shocked, an expression Tj had never associated with the woman.

"It seems Zachary had been trying to contact his dad, so Trent decided to make a detour to meet him," Tj explained.

"Will's still alive?"

"No, I'm sorry, he died a year ago."

Prudence lowered her eyes.

"I know it's none of my business, but after speaking to Trent, I have to admit I was curious about your relationship with Zachary. If Arthur was good friends with him around the time of your wedding, I'm guessing you must have known him back before his accident."

Prudence sat down on one of the stools behind the counter.

Tj waited as a parade of emotions from grief to happiness crossed her face. She looked toward Tj, who could tell she was seeing a memory from her past. A dreamy look come over her face as she began to speak. "Yes, I knew him. I dated him for a while. He was quite a looker, but Will was the one who really caught my eye. Handsome and rugged; not like those pretty boys you girls today seem to prefer. Will was a real man; a bit grizzly, if you know what I mean."

A mental image of Grizzly Adams popped into Tj's head. She wasn't sure if that was what Pru meant, but she decided to remain silent and wait for her to continue.

"When I was a teenager I worked at a little pub on Steamers Wharf. My poor papa nearly popped an artery when I took the job as a bar maid, but it was fun and the money was good, so I stayed on despite his disapproval. It was the best decision of my life. That's where I met Will."

Tj saw a single tear slide down the wrinkled cheek of the suddenly vulnerable woman. She started to take a step forward, but Hazel motioned for her to stay where she was.

"He was working as a deckhand for the summer and we hit it off. We went out a few times before he introduced me to his friends, Arthur, Zachary, and a man by the name of Timothy Bell. I was a real looker back then, if I do say so myself. And—" she looked directly at Tj "—although I hate to admit it, a bit of a tease."

Prudence, a tease?

"It didn't take long before I had all four men wanting to date me. Being young, I didn't see the harm in giving them all a spin. Not that I was a tartlet, mind you."

"No, I'm sure you weren't." Tj hid her smile.

"Not like young girls today who give the milk away before the cow is bought and paid for. No, this keg was only tapped once, but that doesn't mean a gal can't do a little sampling before she hitches her plow to any one horse."

Tj realized Pru must be nervous, the way she was spouting clichés like there was no tomorrow. Not that Pru was above speaking her mind, but she usually was a bit more eloquent in her delivery.

"It was a magical summer, with all four men vying for my attention," Pru continued. "I painted the town red with a different man on my arm each night of the week. We danced and we drank and shared long good-night kisses under the summer moon. It was all so romantic. I hated to see it end, but eventually I realized I had to make a choice, and I chose Arthur. He seemed the most responsible of the four. When she's looking for a husband, a gal looks for a man who will put down roots and return faithfully to the nest every night. Will was the handsomest of the group but also the wildest. I figured a gal like me could never hold him in the long run. After Arthur and I became engaged, Will left and I never saw him again."

"And Zachary?"

"Zachary continued with a life of drinking and chasing girls until he fell in love with a young woman from off the mountain."

"Do you know her name?"

Prudence tapped her lip with her right forefinger. "I never met her, but I believe her name was Mary. I have no idea what her last name was or where she came from. After bringing her home, the couple chose to spend most of their time in his big old house. Folks in town used to speculate about what was going on, but most of it was nothing more than rumor, I suppose."

"Zachary was married?"

Pru shrugged. "Don't really know."

"Do you know what happened to her?"

"I'm afraid I don't. Shortly after the woman came on the

scene Zachary was in the car accident which killed Timothy Bell. I don't remember hearing about a girlfriend or wife after that. Now that I think about it, I'm pretty sure that this Mary was out of the picture before Zachary's accident."

"You know," Hazel joined in, "if you're really interested in this, you might talk to Frannie. The library has a bunch of handwritten journals donated by locals from as far back as the logging camp Zachary's grandfather Jeremiah Collins ran. You might be able to fill in some of the gaps in the story."

"Thanks. I'll do that."

Tj glanced at the clock. If she skipped lunch, she'd still have an hour of her two-hour lunch and prep period left before she had to be back to the school.

The library was just two doors down from the post office, so she headed over to see what she could find out from the documents Hazel had mentioned.

The library was one of Tj's favorite places in town. Built as a bordello at the turn of the century, it had been converted into a library over sixty years ago, a few years after the town was incorporated. The downstairs, which at one time had served as a common room for entertaining, held a large wooden counter that was now used as a reference desk but originally served as the bar on which girls had danced to entertain the men.

Behind the counter were rows of bookshelves holding reference materials that could only be accessed with librarian supervision. In front of the counter was an open area in which round tables surrounded by chairs were provided for patrons.

The upstairs was divided into smaller rooms, converted from bedrooms into bookrooms, each with its own subject matter. One room was decorated in nursery rhymes and held children's books, another housed fiction, yet another reference and business books, and another self-help and religion.

Each bookroom contained long sofas or cozy chairs where visitors could preview a book before checking it out.

"Afternoon, Tj," Frannie, the fifty-six-year-old spinster librarian greeted her. "I'm glad you came in. The book you asked me to track down for one of your students arrived this morning." She adjusted her wire-framed glasses as she held up a hardback book. "*A Mom at Sixteen*?" she queried.

"One of my girls seems to be headed for that. The school counselor recommended the book, but I couldn't find it in the bookstore or online."

"It's been out of print for quite a few years," Frannie explained. "I have a couple of used booksellers who can usually track down what I need. I hope it helps. Sixteen is a little young to be changing diapers and worrying about which brand of formula to buy."

"Tell me about it. The reason I'm here is because I'm researching Zachary Collins's past, and Hazel mentioned you have an archive of old journals and other documents that might help me."

"Hazel was correct; we have a nice collection. I'm afraid they can't be checked out, though. You're welcome to look at things here, if you'd like."

"That's great, but I'm in a bit of a hurry. I'm most interested in finding out what I can about the young woman who lived with Zachary before his accident. In all the years I knew him, he never mentioned her."

Frannie opened a glass-fronted cabinet at the back of the room. "I know exactly the place to start your search. I was sorry to hear about Mr. Collins's death. I didn't really know the man, but anyone who would willingly retreat from the world the way he did must have been living with a great deal of pain. I pray he is finally at peace."

"Yeah, me too."

"These journals were donated by Emma Grainger after her sister, who had the books in her attic, passed away last summer." Frannie pulled one black, leather-bound book from the shelf. "Emma's mother, Isabelle Pritchett, was the local midwife before the hospital opened. She kept a diary for each of the twenty-seven years she lived here. This volume covers 1955 to 1960."

Tj took the journal to one of the round tables in the center of the room and began reading. While the majority of the population of Serenity had moved to the area much later than the time period in which the journal had been written, it was fun to read about the families who originally settled the area.

Her good friend Brock Fisher's grandfather had moved to the area in the early 1930s after establishing a marina where the seasonal steamships that transported the wealthy from one end of the lake to the other could buy supplies and dock for the winter. The marina became known as Steamers Wharf, a name that stuck to this day, despite the fact that it had been many years since the old boats had chugged across the azure waters of Paradise Lake.

The daily lives of many of the founding families were outlined in the well-written pages of the journal. When she had more time she'd have to come back and read about the parents and grandparents of the people she knew, who were now parents and grandparents themselves.

Twenty minutes of skimming later, Tj found what she was looking for.

"The Collins heir has brought home a bride," Isabelle wrote on September 12, 1955. "At least I assume she's a bride. The girl looks barely old enough to have left the care of her parents, yet she seems quite devoted to Zachary. Perhaps this is what he needs to finally settle down and become the man his grandfather would have hoped."

Tj continued to flip through the journal. She gasped when she came to an entry dated March 12, 1956. "I met Zachary's young woman at his estate today. I was called to confirm her pregnancy, which I estimated to be about three months along. Zachary swore me to secrecy regarding the impending birth of his child. I don't understand why he wants to keep the child a secret, but the girl, who gave only the name of Mary, is even younger than I first imagined. She only just turned seventeen, but it seems she has already delivered at least one child. She's a lovely young girl, full of life and hope, but I could tell by her guarded answers that she holds a secret close to her heart."

Zachary had a child? The sound of the old-fashioned wall clock loudly clicked away the minutes in the otherwise silent room. Reading Isabelle's journal was fascinating, but it also felt like peeking into someone's private thoughts. Tj assumed that if Emma had donated the journals to the library, Isabelle must have intended her diaries to be read, unlike Tj's journals, which she hoped no one would *ever* read. Maybe she should rethink keeping them. She'd be mortified if anyone ever read about her schoolgirl crushes or, worse yet, her adult crushes.

Tj paused at an entry she'd almost missed. "Mary's melancholy worsens as the birth of her child grows near. While it is not uncommon for a woman's discontent to grow as the weight of her burden becomes larger, Mary has slipped into a much deeper depression than is normal. I entered into a conversation with her as I checked her progress, and she revealed to me that she wasn't married to Zachary, as most assumed, but still married, in fact, to a traveling preacher with whom she'd born twin daughters the previous year."

And then, on August 17, 1956, she wrote: "Mary will give

birth today. I fear the child will come breach. This pregnancy hasn't been easy for the young girl, and with each hour of labor her strength fades. I held her as she cried for the mistakes she'd made in her life, the daughters she'd deserted, the strict and uncompromising father she barely knew, the much-older man she was married to but never loved."

CHAPTER 17

After school, Tj headed over to see what, if anything, Emma Grainger might be able to tell her about her mother's journals. Grainger's General Store was considered by most to be synonymous with the town of Serenity. First built by Manny Grainger, Nick's father, and later handed down to Nick who ran it with his wife Emma, it had been a staple of the community for over fifty years. On any given summer day, the front deck was occupied by both visitors and locals gathered around to enjoy a game of chess or checkers while sharing a pot of coffee and catching up on local events.

The store was laid out on two stories, the second being open to the first in the center. Wide stairs built at each end of the building gave shoppers easy access to the clothing, camping supplies, and local souvenirs housed upstairs. A seasonal display of bright red sleds, green-handled snow shovels, and black knee-high snow boots were stacked at the base of the stairs under a sign reminding patrons that the first snow of the season was just around the corner.

In the center of the main floor was a square counter with cash registers and glass jars filled with candy that, at Grainger's, still cost a penny. Garlands of bright orange, red, and yellow leaves were draped across the front of the wooden display, while bright orange pumpkins were piled on the surface.

Emma Grainger was standing behind the antique cash

register talking to a customer Tj didn't recognize. She walked across the brightly polished, but heavily scratched and pockmarked, wooden floor toward the front counter. Tj sifted through a table of hand-knitted wool sweaters and warm angora mittens in a variety of bright colors while waiting for Emma to finish her conversation. Perhaps she should get a pair of the dark green ones for Ashley, and maybe the bright red for Gracie. Both girls were going to need waterproof boots and heavy winter jackets as well. Last winter they'd still lived in sunny Los Angeles with their parents. Had it really only been three months since they'd come to Serenity?

"Tj, how are you, dear?" Emma greeted her.

"Do you have a moment?" Tj set the mittens aside, deciding to let the girls pick out their own colors.

"Certainly." Emma waved to a young girl restocking shelves in a gesture indicating she was taking a break. "Let's go back to the office and have a cup of coffee."

Emma poured coffee for both of them, then sat down across from Tj at an old oak table the staff used for breaks. A warm fire crackled cozily in a potbellied stove in the corner of the cheery room while soothing music played softly in the background. "Now, what can I do for you?"

By the time Tj was on her second cup of coffee, she had explained about her search of Zachary's past, the information she'd gotten from Isabelle's journals, and her desire to find out more about Mary's child. She hoped Isabelle had mentioned something to Emma that could help her figure out what happened all those years ago.

"My mother never talked about it," Emma said. "But I do have her official birthing papers. Serenity Community Hospital wasn't built until 1965. Prior to that, anyone with a medical emergency had to go down the mountain to the hospital in

Reno. My mother was a trained midwife and delivered most of the babies in town. She kept files on each of her mothers, much as a doctor would keep a medical file on each patient. The files contained personal information I didn't feel comfortable donating to the library. I've kept them locked up in a chest at home. I'd be happy to see if I can find the file on Zachary's Mary, if you'd like."

"That would be great. I really appreciate your help. The further I dig into Zachary's past the clearer it becomes that I never really knew him."

"It happens that way sometimes."

"By the way, is Tommy around? I had a few questions for him as well."

"He was out doing deliveries but if he has returned you'll most likely find him in the stock room behind the store. You're welcome to check on your way out."

"Thanks. I'll do that."

Tj was lucky to find that Tommy had returned from his deliveries and was busy unpacking inventory. Tommy had just graduated from Serenity High the previous spring so Tj knew him well.

"Hey Coach Jensen. Are you looking for me?"

"Yes. I understand that prior to his death you delivered groceries and other household items to Zachary Collins."

"Yeah, every Friday. I'd deliver the items he'd ordered from the store and pick up his order for the following week. He wasn't as creepy as everyone said. I was sorry to hear that he'd died."

"Did you make a delivery last Friday?"

"Yes ma'am. Right at noon as I always did."

"Did you talk to Zachary when you dropped off his supplies?" Tj asked.

"Not really. I mean I'd say hi and he'd say hi back.

Occasionally he'd comment about a product he'd received that he'd particularly liked or didn't like. If we got new items in at the store that I thought he'd enjoy, I'd mention it. The man was a really good tipper, especially when I did extra errands for him."

"What sort of errands?"

"Once a month, I'd go by the pharmacy and pick up his medications, and every now and then he'd ask me to stop at the bakery."

"Did you ever pick up medication from anywhere other than the pharmacy?"

"No ma'am," Tommy replied. "Mr. Collins did ask me to pick up an order he'd called in to that new store in town that sells cards and gift items last week. It was the first time he'd done that. Most of the time he limited himself to Grainger's General Store, the pharmacy, and the bakery."

"Do you know what he ordered from the new store?"

"No ma'am. It was in a sealed package, and I didn't look."

"Okay, thanks. Have a good day."

As soon as Tj finished speaking to Tommy she called the gift store Tommy had referred to and spoke to the owner who informed her that Zachary had called in an order for a card and wrapping paper. Most likely for the gift she'd found. It made her both happy and sad to know that he'd been thinking of her on the final day of his life. After she hung up she hurried down the street to the sheriff's office for her appointment with Dylan, arriving with less than a minute to spare.

"I have to pick up the girls in less than thirty minutes," Tj began, "but I wanted to talk to you about a few things I've found out."

"Shoot." Dylan leaned forward, giving her his full attention.

"I don't believe Zachary Collins's death was an accident or a suicide," Tj began.

"You think he was murdered?"

"I do."

Dylan paused to consider her assertion. "Do you mind sharing why you think this?"

"I think it has something to do with the house or, more precisely, access to his land. Glen told me Zachary sold the house to Lloyd Benson before he died."

"So?"

Tj outlined the past conversations she had had with Zachary concerning his love for the house his grandfather had built in the eighteen hundreds, and his desire to see it preserved. Zachary had turned down Lloyd's offer to buy the property on multiple occasions.

"So you think Mr. Collins was murdered and this developer had something to do with it?" Dylan asked.

"All I know is it's totally out of character for Zachary to sell the house. He didn't care about much, but he cared about the house and the land it was built on. He told me stories about the banister he slid down as a child, and the way his mother would laugh when he fell at the bottom. He showed me the mantel his grandfather carved from the first tree that fell when he opened his lumber mill, and he told me about the old-growth trees surrounding the estate and his grandmother's adamant refusal to let his grandfather cut even one. Zachary loved that house. I'm certain if he didn't have family to leave it to, he would have left it to the town, or maybe the historical society. Besides, I've also heard that Lloyd applied for a permit to build the condos before Zachary even died, and, according to Glen, one of the stipulations of the sale was that Zachary could continue to live in the house until his death."

"Okay. I'll look in to all of this and see what I can find out. Anything else?"

"Yes. There's a general contractor in town named Kurt Brown. After you left the hardware store yesterday, I overheard Mr. Chase speaking to him on the phone. It seems he's been hired to build Lloyd's condos. Mr. Chase said that before he got the job, Kurt was on the verge of bankruptcy. Mr. Chase also mentioned that Kurt thought he might lose the job due to access issues and was relieved it was back on track."

"You think he could have killed Zachary to save the project?

"I don't know. Maybe."

"I spoke to Kurt Brown after I found out that he had been going around town telling everyone that it was fortunate that Zachary died when he did. It is true that the man believed that Zachary was a potential obstacle to the project he was counting on to get him out of debt, and he didn't seem remorseful about Zachary's death which made him suspect in my mind, but he did have an alibi."

"Alibi?"

"He was at the bowling alley on the night Zachary died. I've verified this with the desk clerk."

Darn. Kurt seemed like a viable suspect. Tj knew that she was going to need to find someone with a real motive to kill Zachary if Dylan was going to take her seriously. Maybe the thing with Lloyd would pan out. Tj glanced at the clock on the wall. "I really should get going. I did want to thank you for being so nice to the girls yesterday. I think they might have little crushes on you."

"They seem like great kids."

"That your nephew?" Tj indicated the photo she'd seen the first time she was in his office.

"Yeah, Justin. I really miss him."

"Did you see him often before you moved out west?" Tj asked.

"Every day. My sister moved in with me after she found out she was pregnant. Her deadbeat boyfriend took off the minute he heard he was going to be a daddy. Allie and I raised Justin together until I got married three years ago. After that, Allie moved into an apartment down the hall, so I still saw Justin every day. He's really more like a son than a nephew."

"Your sister didn't want to move out here with you? You'll certainly have room in that big old house."

"No." Tj saw a flash of pain in his eyes before he changed the subject. "I guess you heard that my wife was killed by gunfire meant for me. It seems to be all over town. After the attack at my apartment Allie refused to let Justin hang out with me any longer. She reasoned that if Justin had been at our place when the man who killed Anna broke in, he might have died as well."

"I heard about how your wife was killed. News travels fast in a small town. I'm so sorry for your loss."

"Thank you. I really don't like to talk about it and it's been hard living in a small town where everyone knows everyone's business, but I'm learning to deal with it. By the way, do you know if Mr. Collins had any documents listing his next of kin? So far we haven't been able to find anyone who knows of any relations, distant or otherwise. I spoke to Mr. Collins attorney and he stated that there were no heirs listed in the will, but I know that you knew him best and perhaps he might have mentioned a distant relative that really should be notified."

Tj thought about the question. Zachary was a loner, he really didn't have anyone, although... "Zachary's family came from England at least three generations ago. I don't know of anyone he stayed in contact with, but when I was participating in one of the scavenger hunts Zachary set up for me to solve when I was a kid, I discovered a book Zachary's dad kept which outlined the family history at least up until his generation, so there should be entries through the late nineteen forties at least. I can get it for you, if you want."

"That would be helpful. Do you have access to the property?"

"I know where Zachary kept the spare key." Tj looked at her watch. "I really have to go. If my friend Jenna can watch the girls, I'll do it this afternoon. I'd planned to start carving pumpkins, but I guess I can put it off until tonight after the haunted house."

"Pumpkins?"

"For the community jack-o'-lantern stroll on Saturday night. In a moment of insanity, I volunteered to carve twenty-five of them."

"I've been known to carve a mean jack-o'-lantern. Drop a few by and I'll see what I can do."

"Wow, that would be so great. Can you do five?"

"When do you need them?"

"By three o'clock on Friday."

"I'm working security for the pumpkin festival tonight, but five should be doable. Drop them by when you have a chance. If I'm not here just leave them in my office."

After Tj picked up both her sisters and Jenna's daughters she dropped off all four girls at The Antiquery. Jenna agreed to let the girls work on their homework in one of the booths while Tj went to Zachary's to look for the family history before the group headed over to the opening night of the festival. Tj once observed Zachary retrieving the key to the cabinet housing his family history from his bedside table. She climbed the stairs, opened the bedroom door, and peeked inside. The sun had begun to set, but the large window overlooking the lake provided enough light for Tj to make out the various pieces of furniture in the room. A four-poster bed, a large hand-carved chest, twin bedside tables, a tall dresser, and an old rocking chair furnished the main part of the room, while a long sofa and two wing-backed chairs were arranged in front of a ceiling-high stone fireplace.

She opened the drawer of the bedside table and searched for the key. Sorting through the contents of such a personal space felt like more of an invasion than Tj was comfortable with. At the bottom of the deep drawer was a box, which she opened to find a stack of black-and-white photos, including one of a young woman Tj realized must be Mary. She stood in front of the Model T, her belly full with child. She was laughing, most likely at something the photographer had said or done. It seemed strange to imagine a younger, more carefree version of the man she had known.

Tj gasped. The woman was wearing the necklace that matched the one Maude and Millie had received from the religious group where they were raised. Tj decided to try to get some additional information from the sisters about the group later, but for now she needed to get the book and then meet Jenna and the girls.

Alongside the photographs were two gold keys. One was most likely for the cabinet, while the other must be for—Tj looked around the room—the chest? She knew she should take the keys and go, but an overwhelming compulsion found her walking across the room to the chest. Slowly inserting the second key, Tj lifted the lid. She placed a hand to her mouth as tears filled her eyes.

The chest was full of items bought for a baby. His baby. A stack of blankets, tiny newborn clothes, and a hand-quilted comforter. "From Life A Gift," Tj whispered.

She thought of the riddle Zachary had left in the puzzle box. Of course. "From life a gift." Zachary must have been referring to his baby. Taking the unsolved riddle of the box out of her purse, she reread the words.

From the ashes of the past
springs new Life as truths reveal
the penance of A sinner
and the Gift put forth to heal

Zachary must have been planning to use the game as a way of sharing his past with her. If the clue in the box led to the next clue in the game, as was the way the treasure hunt usually worked, the answer would be something contained within the house relating to his child.

Tj frowned. Other than the stuff in the chest, she couldn't think of a single thing in the entire house that would relate to a child. Looking around the room, she noticed a small brown teddy bear sitting in one of the chairs facing the old stone fireplace that she'd never noticed before. Picking it up, she found a small piece of paper tucked under the ribbon tied around its neck. The clue read:

The end of past
I'm the first of my kind
And am frozen in time
Of which I am the beginning

Under the phrase were three numbers, 8-18-49.

Tucking the new riddle into her pocket, TJ returned to the living room and the locked cabinet that held the family history, as well as other items from Zachary's past. She inserted the key, then opened the glass door and carefully picked up a large book with leather binding and yellowed pages. A piece of paper fell out of the back as she settled the book into the crook of her arm. Setting the book back down, she unfolded the paper and gasped. If Tj had been surprised to learn that Jeff and Zachary were friends, she was even more stunned to learn that they were related. Tj called Jenna and asked if she could watch the girls a little longer. It seemed that paying a visit to Jeff Warren had taken on a new urgency. Jenna told her that she'd just take all the girls to the festival and Tj could meet them there when she had completed her errands.

Warren Automotive was originally an old barn at the edge of town that Jeff converted into a modest garage with two lifts and a tire center. The large fenced yard behind the garage, which used to hold horses, was now used as a storage facility for those vehicles waiting for parts.

Jeff had earned a solid reputation in the few years he'd been in business, with most folks taking their cars to him for repairs rather than making a trip into the city.

"Hey, Tj." Jeff, a tall, slim man with a mop of thick blond hair and a goofy smile greeted her as he wiped his hands on a greasy rag. "Stella giving you trouble again?" he asked, referring to her seven-year-old 4Runner.

"No, she's still purring like a kitten." Tj stepped over a puddle of oil and sat down on one of the stools set out for customers. "That new exhaust system you installed really makes a difference."

"Glad you like it. I'm trying to get your grandpa to let me put something similar on his truck." Jeff nodded to her grandpa's old Ford sitting in the corner of the garage with a tarp draped over it.

"He's attached to the old girl," Tj said. "Real picky about what's done to her."

"Tell me about it." Jeff smiled. "I tried to get him to let me fix that dent in the bumper as long as I was going to have her here rebuilding the transmission, but he wouldn't hear of it. Said it had sentimental value. Personally, I don't see how a dent can have sentimental value."

"My Grandma Maggie backed into a tree just days after my grandpa bought the truck," Tj explained. "I have no idea why she was driving it, since she was a tiny little thing who couldn't even see out the back window. Grandpa says he and Grandma had a huge fight over it."

"So why didn't he ever get it fixed?"

"The way Grandpa tells it, the bigger the fight, the better the making up."

"Ahhh. Guess I get the sentimental-value part. What can I do for you today?"

"I guess you heard about Zachary Collins." Tj decided to dive right in.

"Yeah." Jeff bowed his head. "I heard. Old Zach was a good man. Not a lot of people knew that, although if anyone did it'd be you. Any word about a funeral? I'd like to pay my respects."

"Not yet." Tj made a mental note to stop by Serenity Community Church later that day to discuss that very subject with Pastor Dan. "I was talking to Greg Remington and he mentioned you were friends with Zachary."

"Yeah, as much as anyone could be friends with the old coot," Jeff said with affection. "My grandpa knew him. I lost my job a few years back and my gramps asked if I'd be willing to spend the summer in Serenity to help out an old friend. I had nothing better to do, and the old guy was payin' well for simple handyman work, so I agreed. Fell in love with the place and have been here ever since."

"And the two of you became friends?"

"Not at first," Jeff admitted. "Dude was a hard nut to crack. There were a couple of times in the beginning when I almost quit outright and headed back home to the Bay. But over time we became friends of a sort, bonded over a common interest. I noticed the photo of that old Model T on the wall in his cellar and we started talking cars. It's always been my dream to restore old classics to their former glory."

"Did you continue to visit after you left his employ?"

"Yeah, every now and again."

"Had you seen him recently?"

"Yeah. In fact, we shared a game of chess just last Friday. Didn't get a chance to finish it, though. Zachary was expecting someone to drop by." Jeff bowed his head again. "Guess we'll never get to finish that game. I'm gonna miss the old guy. You know, he gave me the money to open this place."

"Wow. That was nice of him. Seems like a lot of money to give to a casual acquaintance." Tj watched Jeff's face for a reaction.

"That's what I thought. I offered to repay him when I got the shop on its feet, but he said he didn't want the money back. Said he had more money than he was ever going to need and didn't figure there was any sense in it just sitting around getting dusty when the town needed a good repair shop. He told me to use any profits I got to buy that classic car I was always talking about. Bought a '57 Chevy last year. It's a shame he won't be around to see it when I get it finished."

"You said your grandfather and Zachary were friends. Any idea how they knew each other?" Tj asked.

"Not really. Gramps said something about knowing Zachary from his youth. I guess they stayed in touch."

Tj turned to leave. "When you were visiting Zachary last Friday did you share a meal?"

"Yes. Clam Chowder. Why?"

"No reason."

Tj knew Jenna and the girls were waiting for her but she really did need to find out what was to be done about a funeral, so she made a quick stop at the church to speak with Pastor Dan before heading to the Pumpkin Festival. Serenity Community Church was built in 1951 with a donation from a transplant from New England who thought worshiping the Lord in an abandoned logging mill just didn't have the same effect as attending a pretty little white clapboard church with a traditional steeple. Originally the church had been a single long room with a wide stepped entry leading up to double pine doors. A-frame in shape with a tall bell tower built to mimic those in the East, the small building became a focal point for what would eventually grow into a charming downtown area. Over the years, a wing had been added to the building, as well as a detached community center and local park where picnics were held on a regular basis during the summer months.

"I was going to call you," Dan, a young and strikingly handsome man with longish blond hair and a neatly groomed beard, began as Tj walked toward where he was watering flowers. "The coroner released Zachary Collins's body for burial, so I wanted to talk to you about the service. Do you have a moment?"

"Actually, that's why I'm here. I figured since he didn't have any family I'd try to arrange something."

"How about we go into my office?" Dan opened one of the pine doors, which were always left unlocked for anyone needing refuge. The main room was long and narrow with solid pine floors and rows of sturdy pews built from the same trees that populated the area. At the front of the long room was an altar, less ostentatious than some, with a small pedestal from which sermons could be delivered and a large open area for the choir.

Dan led her down the center aisle, then turned to her left toward the added-on wing that opened into a hallway with a children's room, complete with small tables and chairs and stacks of toys, and several offices, including Dan's.

"Please have a seat." Dan gestured toward a cozy leather sofa and matching chair. "About six weeks ago," he began, "I received a letter from Zachary Collins. The letter, which was accompanied by a rather large donation for the church, detailed a simple but very specific set of instructions to be adhered to upon his death."

"So he knew he was going to die," Tj concluded.

Dan pulled the letter from a file on his desk. "I don't know that he knew the end was going to play out in quite the way it did, but he was an old man in failing health, so, yes, I believe he realized the end was near. In any event, he had a strong-enough inkling to want to put his final affairs in order."

"And his instructions?" Tj asked.

"He requested that he be buried in the family plot with only you in attendance," he nodded toward Tj, "and anyone else *you* deemed appropriate. He specifically stated he did not want a large affair at which self-involved people he had never even met pretended to be saddened by his passing."

"Sounds like Zachary, gruff to the end." Tj smiled sadly.

"I'd like to have the funeral Sunday after services," Dan continued. "If that works for you, of course. Since a community service wasn't requested, there won't be a lot of planning required."

"Sunday will be fine." Sunday was Halloween, and their anniversary. It seemed fitting to say a final farewell on their special day.

"Uh, there's one more thing," Dan said as Tj got up to leave. He handed her a piece of paper.

"This is a birth certificate?"

"It was with the stuff that Zachary left for me."

The certificate was dated in 1956 and listed the baby's name as Baby Boy Collins. According to the signature on the document it had not been Isabella who had delivered the baby but Jake Hanson, a retired doctor now, who would have just moved to the area when Zachary's son was born. Tj called Jake but he was not at home. She knew she'd see him the following day so she headed toward town where she knew Jenna and the girls were waiting to go to the haunted house.

CHAPTER 18

Thursday, October 28

By Thursday the Pumpkin Festival was in full swing and Tj's ability to investigate Zachary's death would be greatly hindered. Of course most everyone in town would be at the event so maybe she could combine the two tasks into one. If nothing else she knew that Jake planned to attend the annual chili cook-off.

"I'm glad you're here." Jenna, dressed casually in a pair of faded jeans, a deep burgundy sweater, and worn Nikes, handed Tj a stack of score cards as soon as she arrived at the cook-off. "My helper is late, so I need you to go around to each entrant and get some basic information. Fill in the top of each card and bring them back to me when you're done."

Tj looked at the card. There was a spot for the name of the entrant, the type of chili, etc. Jenna appeared, as always, in control and pulled together, a personality trait for which she was well known and widely respected, but to the best friend's eye, she seemed more than a little harried despite the fact that not a single blond hair had dared escape the perfectly straight ponytail that hung down her back. "Anything else?"

"Probably. Check with me when you're done. Oh, and Tj—"

"Yeah?"

"We're on a tight schedule, so make it quick."

"Ten four," Tj teased. Deciding to start with the participant closest to the judges' booth and work her way around in a semicircle from there, she turned to her right.

"Hey, guys I need you to fill these out," Tj said, handing an entry card to Carl Osgood, the high school football coach, who was tending a booth along with Nikki.

"Name of chili?" Carl asked as he read the question below the entrant's name.

"Firehouse Special," Nikki suggested.

Carl paused and took a taste of the meaty concoction bubbling in front of him. "Seems about right. Want a taste?" Carl held a spoonful up for Tj to sample as Nikki frantically shook her head in the background.

"Thanks, but I'm supposed to stay neutral in case they need an additional judge," Tj lied. "Right now I just need to get these cards filled out, then report back to Sergeant Jenna."

"How's she holding up?" Nikki laughed. "I guess an even better question is, how are you holding up?"

"Better than at the Christmas pageant." Tj giggled as she remembered being dressed in red tights and a green leotard to play a last-minute elf instead of the teenager who had come down with the flu at a most inopportune time. While the outfit had been completely embarrassing, playing elf to ex-boyfriend Hunter Hanson's Santa had been the most fun she'd had in years.

"If you do end up playing judge today, you might want to take just the tiniest bite of our entry," Nikki warned. "It's so incredibly unique," she added diplomatically, "that you can get the full appreciation of the flavor with just a small taste."

"Kind of like a really good fudge that's so rich you just need a little," Tj added when she noticed Carl's frown.

"Exactly." Nikki sighed in gratitude.

"If you don't get to do the judging gig, come on back and I'll save you a bowl," Carl added. "My chili is like nothing you've ever tasted. I'd hate for you to miss out."

"Can't wait to try it. I'll be sure to come by," Tj promised and continued down the row of entrants.

She tried to relax and enjoy the festive atmosphere: the sound of laughter and screaming in the background as kids of all ages rode the rides provided by the traveling carnival, the smell of spicy chili intermingled with the aroma of kettle corn from one of the portable snack shacks that had been set up around the area. The Pumpkin Festival had always been one of Tj's favorite annual events.

"Hey, Nolan," Tj greeted Nolan Rivers, the next entrant in line and one of her grandpa's oldest friends. Most people thought he was Doc's stiffest competition this year. "I need to get some information for the judges."

"'Kay, shoot." Nolan continued chopping onions as he spoke.

"Let's see, a lot of this I already know," Tj said, writing down his name.

"By the way," Nolan said, as he waited for Tj to finish what she was doing, "I wanted to tell you that I was sorry to hear about Zachary. It's been a while since I've seen the old boy, but I know you were friends."

"You knew him?" Tj looked up from the card she was filling out.

"A long time ago. My dad was friends with Charles, Zachary's father, and I went to his house a few times when I was a kid. The two men shared a common hobby: coin collecting. I always wondered what Zachary did with his dad's collection. I remember hearing it was quite valuable."

"Really?" Zachary had never mentioned a coin collection, but then there were clearly a lot of things they never talked about.

"It was pretty common knowledge that Zachary's dad had a penny worth over fifty thousand dollars, and that was seventy-five years ago. Can't imagine what it might be worth now."

"Fifty thousand dollars? Wow. I wonder if Zachary still had it."

Nolan shrugged, "Who knows? It's been years. He might have sold it."

"I guess. So, what would you say the name of that wonderful-smelling concoction is?" Tj asked.

"Venison Surprise," Nolan answered.

"Really? What's the surprise?"

"The surprise is the secret ingredient that's going to win me the trophy this year." Nolan winked.

She smiled. "Venison Surprise it is."

Tj continued down the line of cook-off hopefuls, filling in the basic information for each one. Hank's entry featured a beer-based broth that was heavy on the beef and light on everything else. Harriet Kramer had chosen to make a unique dish out of chicken and white beans, and Rob's entry was served atop pizza dough and covered with cheese.

"Hey, darlin'," Doc greeted her when she arrived at his booth. "Here to taste the winning entry?"

"Not tasting, just filling out paperwork," Tj said. "Where are Grandpa and Bookman?"

"Over talking to Helen." Doc nodded across the grassy area roped off for the event. "Heading to the carnival later?"

"Wouldn't miss it."

"Good. You can ride the roller coaster with me. Ben said his back can't take the twists and turns, and Bookman already promised to accompany Helen. If you ask me, I think they might be sweet on each other."

"Bookman and Helen?" Tj looked across to the group. Helen had been hanging out at the resort when Bookman was visiting a lot more often lately. Tj hadn't thought anything about it, since Helen had been a close friend of her grandfather's for years, but now that Doc mentioned it, she could see where he might have gotten the idea.

"I wouldn't mention it," Doc cautioned. "I don't think either of them know it yet themselves."

"I won't say anything. What are we calling that inferno in a pot this year?" Doc had a reputation for making his chili hotter than hot.

"You know," Doc said with a chuckle, "I was going to go with Hot and Spicy Chili, but Inferno in a Pot sounds perfect."

"Inferno in a Pot it is." Tj finished filling out the card. "Any more news about the tox screen?"

"Not yet. I'll give you a call as soon as I hear something. The boys in the lab tend to work on their own timetable, and trying to rush them usually results in getting pushed to the bottom of the pile."

"Okay, thanks. And good luck with the contest." Tj started to walk away.

"Don't forget about the roller coaster," Doc reminded her.

"I'll meet you back here after the judging," Tj promised.

"Dr. and Dr. Hanson." Tj smiled fondly as she approached the next booth, where Jake and Hunter Hanson were dicing and chopping and stirring and tasting. Tj and Hunter had been the "it" couple throughout high school, much to his socialite mother's dismay. They'd tried to maintain a long-distance relationship when they'd gone off to different colleges, but when Hunter came home with the daughter of one of his mother's best friends on his arm during their junior year, Tj realized it was long past time to move on.

"How's my girl?" Jake came from around the table and enveloped her in a big bear hug.

"Good, and you?" Tj hugged him back. Other than Hunter, Jake had always been Tj's favorite member of the Hanson family.

"Better every day. You know what they say about men over eighty?"

"Don't ask," Hunter warned as he hugged Tj in turn.

"Aw, you're no fun," Jake complained as he picked up a large wooden spoon to stir his masterpiece.

"Jenna rope you into helping out?" Hunter effectively changed the subject.

"Yeah, but so far no bright-colored tights and scratchy beards," Tj teased.

"Too bad." Hunter laughed. Dark brown eyes almost the same shade as his wavy brown hair sparkled at the memory. "I was rather fond of those tights."

Tj blushed as she remembered sitting on Santa's lap and playfully sharing her Christmas list during an ill-advised moment after everyone had left and she had been waiting for Tyler to pick her up. The moment had started as silly fun shared between friends but had ended up dangerously close to a not-so-silly kiss that Tj suspected would have brought up feelings best left dead and buried. It wasn't like she was still in love with Hunter...exactly. It was more that the goofy grin, soulful eyes, and washboard abs that had attracted her in the first place still had the ability to send her heart beating just a little faster than it normally did.

"What's the name of your chili?" Tj thought it was best to bring her imagination into check.

"Healthy Haven."

"Healthy Haven?"

"A heart-healthy alternative to standard chili," Jake answered.

Tj frowned. "Sounds," she hesitated, "delicious?"

Hunter laughed. "It tastes slightly better than you might imagine, and it's the only version of chili that Grandpa Jake's doctor will let him eat since his heart attack."

"I thought you were his doctor?" Tj pointed out.

"I am."

"More like a mother hen, if you ask me. Boy needs to find the right girl, settle down and have a few kids of his own. Maybe then he'll stop coddling me. I heard you were back on the market," Jake hinted.

Tj laughed. "Single, maybe; back on the market, definitely not." She smiled at the man who, if things had worked out differently, might have become her grandfather by marriage. Sometimes Tj wondered what it would have been like to become a Hanson. Her life would certainly have turned out differently if she'd married Hunter. His mother would have tried to turn her into some dainty socialite who would fit in with her high-society friends.

"Can I talk to you for a minute?" Tj asked Jake.

"What's on your mind?"

"Alone," she said, glancing at Hunter.

"Be back in a minute." Jake turned toward Hunter. "Need to have a word with your girl."

"I'm not his girl," Tj said.

"She's not my girl," Hunter said in unison.

Jake just chuckled as he placed Tj's hand on the crook of

his arm and led her away. She knew Jake had been as disappointed over their breakup as Hunter's mother had been thrilled by it. She and Hunter hadn't been a couple for six years, but Tj suspected Jake still hoped they'd patch things up.

"What's on your mind?" Jake asked when they found an isolated spot to talk.

"I wanted to ask about Zachary Collins's baby."

Jake hesitated. "Old Zach told you about that, did he?"

"No," Tj admitted. "It's sort of a long story, but I ran into a guy whose dad knew Zachary. Our conversation brought up some questions, so I started asking around. I found entries in Isabelle's journals in which she talks about Zachary's Mary and the baby she carried, but I couldn't find anything that revealed what became of the child. I know Isabelle was the local midwife but Pastor Dan has a birth certificate for Baby Boy Collins which is signed by you."

"I was a young doctor, new in town, fully licensed but not practicing medicine yet, when Zachary's son was born. I met the midwife, Isabelle, shortly after settling in. She called me on the day Zachary's Mary went into labor. The child was coming breach, and the umbilical cord had become wrapped around the little guy. Mary had lost a lot of blood and didn't have the energy to deliver the baby on her own. Without a C-section, they both would have died."

Tj frowned. "C-section? You operated on her?"

"I did what I had to do. Unfortunately, I didn't have the proper equipment or drugs to safely perform the surgery. Mary begged me to do what I had to do to save the child. She endured a lot so the boy could live."

"You operated without anesthesia?"

"I didn't have time to get her down the mountain to the hospital. The baby was in a great deal of distress by the time I arrived. I made a split-second decision to save the baby, as the mother asked. After he was delivered I tried unsuccessfully to save the mother."

"Oh, God." Tj paled.

"The very next day I vowed to find the money to open a hospital in Serenity. If I had had the resources that a hospital could provide, I could have saved them both."

"And the baby?"

"A healthy baby boy. Zachary was about as distraught as I've ever seen a man. He asked Isabelle to find the baby a good home. I encouraged him to reconsider but he was too distraught to deal with the child who, I believe at the time, he blamed for Mary's death."

"It wasn't the baby's fault."

"I know that, and I think he realized it later."

"Do you know who adopted him?"

"A family by the name of Donovan. I don't know much more about them than that." Jake looked over toward the table where Hunter was stirring ingredients into the chili. "I should get back before the boy destroys our entry. Don't tell him, but I seasoned the ground turkey with beef lard."

"Don't worry, I won't tell." Tj laughed. "And thanks."

Tj handed the information cards to Jenna and apologized for deserting her, but suddenly she needed to talk to Dylan.

CHAPTER 19

"Dylan in?" Tj asked the receptionist at the sheriff's office.

"Deputy Caine is on duty at the Pumpkin Festival."

Darn. She could have saved herself a trip if she'd called first. With all the running around she was doing today, she should have worn her Nikes.

The park where the event was taking place was nestled cozily between the highway and the lake. Fast-food stands, along with rows of picnic tables, were lined up along the grassy lakeshore. Beyond the food court were rows of craft vendors and local service booths. The hayride, pumpkin patch, carnival rides, and hay bale maze had been set up on the high school playing fields. The town had hired a crossing guard to ensure that everyone made it from one section of the festival to the other in a safe and orderly fashion.

After circulating among the craft tables as well as the midway section without a single sighting of Deputy Caine, Tj headed back to the food court and grabbed a bite to eat. The thought of her upcoming roller-coaster ride with Doc made her pause, but in the end hunger won out and she headed for the BBQ Shack where she found Dylan chowing down on his own beefy sandwich.

"Inspector Jensen," Dylan teased. "What brings you by today?"

"New suspects."

"Okay, who are we suspecting now?"

"Jeff Warren."

"That nice guy who fixed my turn signal for no charge the other day?"

"He's a nice enough guy, but he's also related to Zachary Collins."

"Related?"

"According to his book, Zachary's grandfather, Jeremiah Collins, had a brother named Charles. Charles had a dalliance in his youth that resulted in the birth of a bastard child, Jordan. Jordan was Jeff's great-grandfather. Based on the letter I found, Charles disowned the boy in order to appease his aristocratic wife, so Jeremiah brought him to America and gave him a place to live and, eventually, an education. At some point Jordan moved to San Francisco, where the family has lived ever since. The letter indicated Zachary was the one responsible for bringing Jeff to Serenity in the first place. I found a series of letters between Zachary and Jeff's grandfather Ian. It looked like Ian wrote to Zachary and asked if he could help Jeff out. I guess the family was going through some hard times financially. Zachary agreed to do it, and Jeff's grandfather sent him to Serenity to do some repair work for an old friend. At some point Zachary offered Jeff the money to start his business, and he accepted it."

"Do you think Jeff knows they're related?"

"If he does, he's not admitting it."

"Then why would Jeff kill him?" Dylan asked.

"I have no idea, but in my book, everyone's a suspect until proven otherwise. Besides, Jeff admitted to being at Zachary's house on the night he died. They shared a meal and a game of chess, which Jeff did say they were unable to finish since Zachary was expecting someone else to drop by."

"So Jeff can't be the killer."

"Unless he's lying about the someone else."

Dylan frowned. "Okay. So who else are we suspecting?"

"A guest at the resort: Kyle Donovan."

"The same Kyle Donovan with the bottle?"

"Yes, although that lead didn't really pan out. It seems he really did buy the bottle."

"Okay, so what did this Kyle do this time to earn him a spot on your suspect list?"

"He's Zachary's grandson."

"Grandson?"

Tj explained everything she'd learned from Trent, Prudence, Isabelle's journals, Jake and Pastor Dan. "According to Jake, the couple Isabelle found to adopt Zachary's infant son had a last name of Donovan. Kyle's last name is Donovan. I figure he's too young to be Zachary's son, so he must be his grandson."

"Or some random guy with the last name Donovan," Dylan pointed out.

"Really?" Tj asked sarcastically

"I'm not sure I'm buying the spurned grandson scenario."

"Why? He seems like an obvious choice."

"Actually, I had a chat with Kyle after you called me the first time about the bottle. He said he checked into Maggie's Hideaway around three. After getting settled in his cabin, he headed over to the lodge, where he met and talked to you. After that he went to the resort bar, where he enjoyed a basket of buffalo wings and a couple of beers before going back to his cabin for an early night."

Tj nibbled on the end of one of her garlic fries. "So?"

"So how did he kill Zachary if he never left the resort?"

"Good point. I can verify Kyle was in the lodge reading

during the afternoon. He was an instant hit with my dog Echo, who normally doesn't approach guests, so we chatted for a while and then he left. I guess that was around five." Tj dipped her fry in a puddle of ketchup, swirling it around before plopping it in her mouth. "I remember my grandfather saying Kyle helped him decorate the bar that evening, so I guess it sounds like he has an alibi, but still, him being in town for a job interview with a company no one has ever heard of is suspicious."

"I looked into the job interview thing," Dylan confirmed. "He has a letter from a company called The Repository offering him the job. There was a phone number on the letter that simply rang into an answering service. The woman who answered confirmed that the service was being paid to take phone messages for the firm in question. I'm having the service contract sent over."

Tj waved at a group of her students who had gotten in line at the frozen candy bar stand. "Did the people at the answering service say what the person who ordered the service looked like? It could just be Kyle covering his butt."

"They said the service was hired via phone." Dylan took a sip of his soda. "They were paid in advance with a wire transfer authorized by a Mr. Henry. I've been doing this for a long time and I've developed an instinct as to who's lying and who's telling the truth. Kyle didn't say anything that would lead me to believe he knew of his connection to Zachary Collins. He seemed relaxed and forthright during the entire interview. If you want my gut instinct on this, I think he's exactly who he says he is, a guy in town looking for a job. If what you say about Kyle being Zachary's grandson is correct, my guess is that Zachary used the job interview to get Kyle into town for some reason known only to him. Maybe to finally meet him after all these years."

"But he dies before he can schedule the meeting," Tj

realized. She sat back and listened to the sounds of the carnival in the background. So many people going about their lives as if nothing had happened. Zachary was an old man who had lived a long life. She knew she shouldn't feel so bad, but somehow the fact that Zachary had died without knowing either his son or his grandson made her want to cry.

"Are you okay?" Dylan asked.

"Yeah." Tj sighed. "Zachary and I had been friends for a long time. I just want to know what happened to him."

"Don't worry." Dylan placed his hand over hers. "If someone hurt him, we'll figure out who."

CHAPTER 20

Friday, October 29

The next day things were busier than ever at the resort. Leiani called asking for help covering the registration desk before Tj even had her first cup of coffee, denying her the opportunity to analyze what she'd learned the last few days. She promised to call someone in to relieve her, but it was midafternoon and no one had shown up so far. Luckily Dennis stopped by and picked up the pumpkins she and the girls had carved the previous evening, so at least she didn't have to worry about making it into town by three.

Normally Tj didn't mind helping out at the resort, but on this Friday she felt she should be doing something else. She was sure someone had killed Zachary, but who? Lloyd Benson was really her only suspect, and he was a weak suspect at that. Although, he was a large, formidable man who had a moose head hanging in his living room. He *seemed* the type who could be a killer, and he'd wanted Zachary's land for years. Could killing him have been the only way to get it?

Tj's gut told her that she'd find her answers in the clues

Zachary had left. She knew there was no empirical reason to believe this, but her gut was rarely wrong. She retrieved the most recent note from her purse and reread the clue.

The end of past
I'm the first of my kind
And am frozen in time
Of which I am the beginning
8-18-49

"The end of past" would be the present, and "first of my kind" could refer to an individual. "Frozen in time" could be a photograph. Tj frowned. She studied the numbers. Could they belong to a safe of some type? Although Tj didn't have any direct knowledge of a safe, the Collins family had been extremely wealthy. It made sense they'd have a safe somewhere.

Tj thought about the house. The mansion was filled with original artwork Tj suspected was worth hundreds of thousands of dollars. Could there be a safe behind one of those paintings? Maybe once someone showed up to relieve her at reception she'd head to the house and see what she could find. If there was a safe hidden somewhere in the mansion, she intended to find it.

Later that afternoon, Tj drove to the house, letting herself in with the spare key. She slowly opened the door and walked through the house to the living room, looking around as she traveled.

In the movies the safe was always behind a picture in the office. Did Zachary even have an office? The house was huge, but Zachary only used a few of the rooms, leaving the others closed off. It would take hours to search the entire property. If the numbers were a combination to a safe, the riddle must be a clue to point to its location.

> The end of past
> I'm the first of my kind
> And am frozen in time
> Of which I am the beginning

Tj stared at the riddle again. Something about it looked familiar. Zachary had given her a riddle once before with words like "beginning" and "end." In that instance the answer had been a letter. "End of past" was T, as was the beginning of "time." "The first of my kind"?

"Oh, my god, it's the car," Tj said out loud.

Tj headed toward the cellar. "First of my kind" had to refer to the picture of the Model T in the basement. Zachary had told her that when his father bought it, it was the first of its kind, fresh off the assembly line in 1908. "Frozen in time," the next clue, must be associated with the photo.

Turning on the light, she crossed the room to the photo. She lifted it from the wall and found the safe. Using the numbers at the bottom of the clue, 8-18-49, she opened it. Inside the safe was a box with her name on it, and inside the box was a beautiful sapphire-and-diamond necklace Zachary had once told her had belonged to his mother. Beside the necklace was a keno ticket with a phone number written on the back, a gold key, and a small bundle of hundred-dollar bills.

Tj slid the necklace, the keno ticket with the phone number, and the key inside her purse. She left the money where it was, locked the safe, and put the picture back in its place.

Now what? She was supposed to meet Jenna, Dennis, and the girls at the Pumpkin Festival in a half hour. She supposed she should go. Normally she loved the festival, but this year she was too distracted to enjoy it. Deciding to stop by and talk to Dylan on the way, she called Jenna and told her she'd be late, then headed to the car. She was pulling onto the highway when her phone rang. It was Doc, and he had news.

CHAPTER 21

"Who's the date?" Tj glanced across the crowded restaurant where Doc had asked her to meet him. A considerably younger attractive woman waited at the table from which he had just excused himself.

"Cute young thing who just opened that sandwich shop down by the park." Doc stuck out his chest like a rooster strutting his stuff.

"Why, you old dog." Tj smiled at the Casanova of her grandfather's group. "I'm betting she's not a day over fifty."

"Fifty-six," Doc corrected. "She's kept herself together real nice."

"You said you had news?"

"Tox screen confirms that Zachary died of a drug cocktail, as suspected." Doc lowered his voice, even though the music was loud and they were sitting in a private booth in the back of the room. "What's unusual is that the particular blend of narcotics used isn't found in any commercially produced sedative."

"Come again?" Tj asked.

"The drug used to kill Zachary was a custom blend, most likely bought from a street dealer."

"You mean an illegal drug?" Tj clarified.

"Exactly. This particular blend is sort of like a signature, so

I'm thinking we're looking at one of the bigger dealers you'd find in Indulgence, or even Reno," Doc added.

"Any idea how we can track down the dealer who sold it?"

"We can't," Doc said. "And I think we should turn this over to the sheriff's department."

Tj finally had her proof that Zachary was murdered. There was no way he drove to Reno or Indulgence to buy a designer drug. The man didn't even own a car.

"Okay, but Dylan, not Sheriff Boggs. I want to be sure this information doesn't get buried. If we can figure out who bought the drug, we can figure out who killed Zachary."

"I'll forward the information to Deputy Caine as soon as I'm done here," Doc promised.

After calling Jenna, briefly explaining the situation, and arranging for the girls to spend the night at her house after they returned from the Pumpkin Festival, Tj decided to stop by the sheriff's department to see if Dylan was still around. Arriving at the office, she walked in the front door to find the lobby empty. Walking down the narrow hallway, she heard voices coming from Dylan's office.

"That's awesome, buddy," she heard Dylan say.

Tj stopped just outside the door, not wanting to intrude if Dylan had a visitor.

"I knew you'd like it," he continued after a brief pause.

Tj realized that Dylan must be on the phone and, from the sound of it, he was most likely having a personal conversation. Tj turned to go back down the hall toward the lobby when she heard his voice change from jovial to sad.

"I know." His voice caught briefly. "I miss you too."

Tj knew she should leave Dylan to his conversation but

found herself inching closer to his office. She pressed herself against the wall and peeked in through the partially open door. Dylan was sitting at his desk dressed in casual clothes rather than his usual uniform, holding a photo.

"But hey," Dylan said, forcing a smile, "I talked to your mom a few days ago and she said it might be okay for all of us to go to Hawaii again this summer. We had fun there."

Tj realized the photo Dylan was holding was probably the one of him and his nephew Justin at the beach.

"No, Kiva can't come. She wouldn't like the plane ride."

Dylan ran his thumb over the surface of the photo, as if trying to commit to memory every detail of the young boy to whom he was talking. "Yeah, I know you miss her. Tell you what, I'll talk to your mom after I get settled in and see if we can't meet somewhere closer. Maybe somewhere along the California coast." Dylan leaned his head back against the headrest of his chair and closed his eyes as he listened to the person on the other end of the phone line. "I love you too. Have a fantastic birthday tomorrow."

Dylan pinched the bridge of his nose. "I know. Maybe next year."

Tj backed down the hall as quietly as she could. She waited until the red light on the switchboard, indicating that the phone in Dylan's office was in use, went dark, then slammed the front door as loudly as she could.

"Anyone here?" she called.

She heard footsteps in the hallway as Dylan came out to greet her.

"Casual Friday?" Tj asked after Dylan walked into the lobby in stonewashed jeans and a red cable knit sweater.

"Actually, Roy is feeling better, so he's agreed to be on call, giving me the night off." Dylan appeared to be back to his carefree self. "I thought I'd grab a bite to eat, then head home and watch an old movie with Kiva."

"If you have a few minutes, I wanted to talk to you about the results from the tox screen Doc ran."

"Sure, let's head back to my office. The information just came through here, but I haven't had a chance to look at it yet. How did you know about it?"

"I ran into Doc earlier and he told me about it." Tj explained the signature drug angle as Dylan looked over the emailed information. "I was hoping you could track down the dealer who sells this unique blend. Maybe if we find the dealer, we can find our killer."

Dylan frowned. "I'm new around here, so I have no idea who is dealing what in this area, but I knew dealers in Chicago with custom blends and the narc guys had a good handle on who was dealing what. I'll put in a call to the narcotics department in Indulgence and see what they can turn up. In the meantime, care to join me for a bite to eat? I hate to eat alone, and takeout in my hotel room every night is getting pretty old."

"Really?" Tj asked, surprised the handsome deputy would ask her out. "I mean yes, I'd love to."

"By the way, I have something for you." Dylan stopped her. He pulled a large envelope out of his top desk drawer and handed it to her. "I found it at the Collins place. I thought you'd want to have it."

Tj opened the envelope. Inside were old newspaper clippings of her as a teenager and as an adult. There were articles and pictures of all the most important moments of her life, both happy and sad. She couldn't believe Zachary had kept all of these.

There were pictures of her in black and gold as she cheered the various Serenity High School teams to victory; others of the car wash she'd organized in the ninth grade, when the local animal shelter ran short of funding and it looked like it might have to close. There was even a picture of her receiving her diploma at her high school graduation.

Dylan got up from his chair and walked around the desk to stand behind her as she thumbed through pictures of her skiing to victory the year she'd won the regional downhill championship; kicking the winning goal the year the girls' soccer team made it to the state championships; and a god-awful photo of her running across the finish line at last year's Patriot's Day Triathlon.

"That one is my favorite," Dylan commented.

"Seriously? My hair is frizzy from the swim, my face is burned from the sun, and my cheek is smudged with dust from the mountain bike ride."

"The photo is perfect. It's totally you."

"Thanks a lot," Tj groaned as Dylan leaned in over her shoulder.

"Your hair does have a bit of the cave woman thing going on, and the dust on your cheek is noticeably marred with streaks of dried sweat."

"Not helping," Tj growled.

"But look at your smile. You look so happy. Your whole face is glowing, and not just from the sunburn."

Dylan had a point. She did look happy, and there was something empowering about the way her head was tilted back and her arms were raised in victory. While she had always aspired to look a bit more polished, the photo did seem to accurately capture the real Tj Jensen; a five-foot-two half-pint who'd challenged women half a foot taller and clawed her way to victory based on grit and determination alone.

*   *   *

After forwarding the report to the office in Indulgence, and locking the office door behind them, the pair made the short walk down the street to Pops for a bite to eat. Pops was a local joint with a limited menu but excellent food. Tj thought about continuing their conversation about Zachary, but somehow the more intimate atmosphere in the restaurant made this feel like a date.

"How do you like our little town so far?" she asked instead.

"I like it. The scenery is beautiful, the people seem friendly and the work seems a lot slower paced than what I was used to in Chicago. Once we get settled into the new house, I think Kiva and I will like living here just fine."

"Do you ski?"

"Snowboard, actually, but yeah, I enjoy a day on the slopes. Roy mentioned you coach the high school team."

"I coach the downhill team in the winter, soccer in the fall, and track in the spring. I love my job. Working with the kids is both rewarding and very challenging."

"What can I getcha?" Pop said, interrupting their conversation. A large man with a precision military haircut and extensive tattoos covering both arms, Pop had first learned to cook in the army, serving rations to men in the field.

"Could we have a menu?" Dylan asked.

"No menus. Got fried chicken, sirloin steak, meatloaf, or pork chops. Everything comes with mashed potatoes and gravy, homemade biscuits, and green beans. Soup is vegetable beef, salad is mixed greens, and both are included. What's it going to be?"

Dylan frowned.

"I know it sounds like a heart attack on a plate, but trust me when I tell you it's worth it," Tj assured him. "Pop makes the best biscuits and gravy this side of anywhere."

"Okay, I guess I'll take the steak."

"And I'll have the meatloaf." Tj smiled.

"Soup will be right out." Pop walked back toward the kitchen.

Tj and Dylan went on to discuss water sports and the merits of wake surfing versus wake boarding. She told him about the resort and her decision to move back in with her dad after she was granted custody of her two half-sisters. Dylan filled her in on his plans for the house he just bought, and Tj suggested local contractors who could help him with his project. She also told him about the school where she taught and the people she worked with, the usual stuff of first conversations and getting to know each other.

Things got slightly more personal as Dylan shared that he'd grown up in a small town before landing the job in Chicago shortly after his sister, Allie, had given birth to his nephew Justin.

He talked about those first years in Justin's life and how he'd been a part of his daily routine. He'd worked hard and gained recognition, eventually moving the whole family to the big city where he'd met his wife, Anna. He talked about the demands of his new job and losing sight of what was really important, like school plays, Little League games, and romantic nights out with the wife with whom he'd shared a life for such a short time.

Tj wasn't sure how you could ever get over something like the brutal and violent death of your wife. Dylan had shared so much and she wanted to reply in kind, so she shared how difficult the transition from single woman without a care in the world to guardian of two grade-school-aged girls had been. She opened up about her doubts and fears as they related to the twists and turns she knew were ahead as they navigated a life together. She was in the middle of telling him about her breakup with Tyler when Dylan's phone rang.

"It's from the Indulgence Office." Dylan looked at the caller ID. "I should get this."

CHAPTER 22

"Looks like our dealer is a guy who goes by the name of Boots," Dylan informed her.

"Boots?"

"That's what my contact said. Anyway, he said we're most likely to find him working the Strip after the clubs open at nine. He offered to pick him up for questioning, but the personal approach might get us better results. I thought I'd head around the lake and see if I can hook up with the guy."

"Have you ever been down to Indulgence?" Tj asked.

"No, I haven't had the opportunity."

"You'll need a guide. The girls are spending the night at my best friend's, so it just so happens I'm available to come along and serve in that capacity."

Dylan hesitated.

"Come on, Dylan. I know the town like the back of my hand. I can help."

"Okay, but you hang back and do exactly what I say."

"Deal."

The trip around the narrow mountain road that connected the north and south shore of Paradise Lake took about forty minutes. During the daylight it was a beautiful drive, passing white sand beaches, beautiful waterfalls, and evergreen forests.

During the evening the reflection of the bright moon shimmering on the glassy water lent an atmosphere of calm serenity. Tj just wished she could enjoy it.

"Did you ever question Lloyd?" Tj asked.

Dylan nodded. "It turns out he left for Reno on Thursday and didn't return until Sunday."

"Reno's only an hour away," Tj pointed out. "He could have come back, killed Zachary, then returned to finish out the weekend."

"I thought of that. He had a keno ticket with a date and time stamp from a casino on the strip. Seems he's a regular."

"There's no way to tell if he was the one who bought the ticket. He could have had someone do it for him."

Dylan smiled. "Maybe you should have been a cop instead of a teacher. You certainly think like one."

"Are you kidding," Tj laughed. "Where do you think I learned my investigative skills? There's no one who can lie like a teenager. Believe me when I tell you, I've heard it all."

"The possibility of Lloyd returning from Reno to kill Zachary occurred to me. I'm having the surveillance tapes from the casino pulled for the date and time in question."

"Did you ask him about the condo development?"

"He said Glen Keller approached him about a month ago. According to Lloyd, Glen told him Zachary had reconsidered and was ready to sell. Glen handled all the paperwork and Lloyd never even needed to meet with the man who had been a thorn in his side for years."

"Seems odd."

"Maybe, maybe not. Real estate transactions are handled by professional representatives and electronic signatures all the time. Lloyd claims to have a signed document, so if he's lying we'll need proof."

"If Lloyd was in Reno and Kyle was at the resort, who does that leave us? Jeff?"

"I talked to Jeff. He didn't do it," Dylan said. "I found out something new, though I haven't quite decided if it's relevant."

"What?"

"I tracked down the man who ordered the answering service for The Repository. His name is John Henry. He's a private investigator who works out of San Jose. He said Zachary hired him to run a few personal errands and to track down four people."

"Timothy Bell and Kyle," Tj guessed, remembering Trent Jackson had mentioned that a man named John Henry had been looking for Timothy Bell's widow. "Who are the other two?"

"He didn't mention Timothy Bell," Dylan said. "Hang on, I wrote down the names." Dylan managed to fish a folded-up piece of paper from his pocket and handed it to Tj.

She looked at the list, then read it aloud. "Maude and Millie Morrison, Carmen Lewis, and Kyle Donovan." Tj frowned. "We know Zachary figured out Kyle was his grandson and brought him here, but why the other three?"

"Henry didn't say, but I got the feeling he knew. I thought I'd try to track down the names and see what I can find out."

"You won't have to look far. Maude, Millie, and Carmen are all at the resort. They arrived on the same day as Kyle. Zachary must have brought them all here, though I have no idea why. Do you have contact information for John Henry?" Tj asked.

"Yeah, but it won't do you any good. He was headed south of the border on some bounty-hunting job. Said there wouldn't be cell service. He indicated he hoped to be back in a week or two if his lead panned out."

"Figures."

By the time they arrived at the outskirts of the much larger city on the south shore of Paradise Lake it was almost eleven o'clock.

"It looks like a mini Vegas," Dylan commented as they drove through the area known as the Strip, where casinos, nightclubs, and other forms of adult entertainment were located.

"It's a tenth of the size, but the same atmosphere. If you head farther down the road, there's a nice village at the base of the Thunder Mountain ski area with tons of shopping, five-star dining, and luxury hotels; then beyond that is Old Town, with historic buildings, mom-and-pop shops, and a local museum. That's where the county offices are located. I can show you where the main branch of the Paradise County Sheriff's Office is for future reference."

"Thanks, that would be helpful."

"It's probably best to park in one of the casino garages," Tj said. "The Strip is flashy but less than a mile long. We can park and walk the area. Chances are this Boots will be close by if he's working tonight."

Tj pointed Dylan to the parking garage at the Empress, the largest casino on the Strip. "How do you want to play this?" she asked.

"Play this?"

"Yeah, what's our cover?"

"Our 'cover' is that you are a woman out for a walk who is going to hang back while I talk to this guy. Remember our deal?"

"Fine."

Tj sighed. She couldn't remember the last time she'd had so much fun. She loved her sisters and would do anything for them, but until this moment she hadn't realized how truly routine and unexciting her life had become. Playing undercover cop with

Dylan was the most excitement she'd had in a long time.

Dylan parked the truck, locked it, then took Tj by the hand as they exited the parking garage and strolled nonchalantly down the street. Tj's heart skipped a beat as Dylan's large hand closed over her small one. It had been a while since she'd had any male contact with someone she wasn't related to, and Dylan's hand engulfing hers felt better than she'd like to admit.

Tj wasn't a gambler and rarely spent time in casinos, but somehow, strolling down the street hand in hand with a gorgeous man, she felt energized. The atmosphere along the strip was electric with flashing lights and partially drunk pedestrians talking and laughing. If she let her imagination take over just a bit, it almost felt like they were on a date.

Dylan stopped in front of a brightly lit club with loud music vibrating through the doorway. "Guess we'll start here."

The club was smoke filled and dimly lit. Bar top tables surrounded by backless stools faced a small stage where exotic dancers entertained the crowd between eleven and two. The patrons were mostly men in small groups pounding down drinks and flirting with scantily clad cocktail waitresses.

"What now?" Tj whispered.

"You don't need to whisper. The music in here is loud enough that no one would hear you if you shouted."

Tj looked around the room. There was a large group of young men sitting in one corner with several of the waitresses perched on their laps. A dozen or so tables were occupied. Dylan sat Tj down at the bar and ordered her seltzer water, then sauntered over to a table near the stage that was occupied by three women. Tj couldn't hear what they were saying, but she wasn't sure she liked the way all three were leaning forward provocatively to show off their assets.

Dylan made his way around the room, speaking briefly to

each of the patrons. She didn't know if he was getting any leads, but it looked like he was having fun. She hadn't necessarily pegged Dylan as a party animal, yet he seemed right at home in this smoky room dripping with sexual energy. Eventually he returned to the bar where Tj waited.

"Strike out?" Tj asked.

"Three phone numbers." He grinned.

"That's not what I meant."

"I know. Apparently no one in the room knows who this Boots is. And if they do, they aren't talking. Let's take a walk down the Strip. Maybe we'll get lucky."

Dylan took Tj's hand again as they walked past bars, brightly lit gentlemen's clubs, and adult bookstores. A woman dressed in a short skirt, four-inch heels, and a halter top bumped into Tj as they turned the corner toward a small, crowded players' club.

"Sorry." The woman smiled at Dylan, completely ignoring Tj. She must be freezing, Tj thought, as Dylan smiled back at her.

"No problem." Dylan turned on the charm, practically undressing the woman with his eyes. If this had been a real date, Tj would be as mad as hell. "My friend and I are looking for a little something to set the mood. Heard a man who goes by the name of Boots is the one to talk to." Dylan leaned in close to the woman, who seemed to melt right in front of Tj's eyes.

"Boots usually works the park. If you get bored with your friend, give me a call." The woman pulled a short pen out from between her perky double Ds and wrote a number on Dylan's hand. "Just ask for Star."

"Jeez, did you have to be *so* nice to her?" Tj asked after he thanked the woman and walked in the direction she indicated.

"Jealous?"

Tj snorted. "No. I've just never felt quite so invisible before. She didn't know we aren't really a couple."

"Don't think she cared." Dylan walked into a Starbucks.

"Are we stopping for coffee?"

He sat her down at one of the tables near the counter. "*You're* stopping for coffee. I'm going to have a chat with our friend Boots. I shouldn't be too long. Do you have your cell?"

"Yeah, why?"

Dylan took her phone and punched in his number. "Call if you have any problems, and Tj..."

"Yeah?"

"Stay put and don't talk to anyone."

"Yes, Dad."

Tj wasn't thrilled about being left behind, but a latte would be wonderful, and she *had* promised Dylan she'd do everything he said. If she knew she was going to be stuck in a coffee shop by herself, though, she would have brought a book. After ordering her drink, she rummaged around in her purse for something to keep her occupied while she waited for him to return.

Tears welled in her eyes as she spotted the necklace Zachary left her. She knew the necklace had belonged to his mother. She'd noticed it in the cabinet where he kept his most prized keepsakes and commented on how much she liked it. He'd told her he might give it to her one day. Tj took off the necklace she'd been wearing, and slipped the necklace Zachary had given her around her neck. She clasped it behind her head.

Taking out the gold key she'd found, she studied it. It was small with the number seventy-two stamped onto the head. It could open a desk or cabinet, but the number led Tj to believe it was a key used to open something with multiple units, such as a locker or perhaps a safety deposit box.

Tj doubted Zachary actually intended for her to find it;

otherwise he would have left instructions on how to use it. On the other hand, the fact that the riddle led to the safe where the key was kept was odd. If the necklace was the prize at the end of the game, why not hide it in the cookie jar or under a sofa cushion? Why the safe?

The only other item in the safe had been the keno ticket. Another oddity. Zachary never left the confines of his house, and she was certain he wouldn't be spending time in a crowded casino.

The ticket was from a casino on the strip in Reno. Could it have come from Lloyd? And if so, why had he given it to Zachary? The ticket had no monetary value, so Tj figured the phone number was the reason the ticket was in the safe.

Tj tried calling the number.

"Serenity Bowl," someone from the local bowling alley answered.

Why would Zachary have a phone number to the bowling alley in his safe? She remembered the key. Maybe the key went to one of the bowling lockers kept for regulars. Kurt hung out at the bowling alley and had, in fact, used his presence there as his alibi.

"Hi, I'm calling to inquire about your lockers," Tj improvised. "Are they combination locks or do they open with keys?"

"Combination, but they're all rented out. We have a waiting list, if you'd like."

"Uh, no thanks. Do you happen to know a man by the name of Zachary Collins?"

"Old guy who died?"

"Yeah."

"Nah, man. Never met him. Heard the dude never came out of that big, spooky house of his."

"I found a piece of paper with the phone number for the bowling alley in his home. Is there anyone else he might have spoken to?"

"Guess you can ask Terry. He owns the place. Should be tending bar in the grill. I can connect you."

"Thanks, I'd appreciate it."

Terry claimed he had never met or spoken to Zachary. The only other employees at the bowling alley were a middle-aged man named Conway, who also denied knowing Zachary, and a janitor who wouldn't be on duty for another two hours.

Tj was debating what to do when Dylan walked into the coffee shop.

"So?" Tj asked.

"Boots, who by the way wears military fatigues with red cowboy boots—"

"Hence the name," Tj guessed.

"Admitted after a fairly lengthy conversation," Dylan continued, "that he had sold that particular drug cocktail to several people whose names he couldn't remember. When I pulled out my badge and threatened to take him in for dealing, he conveniently remembered that a regular named Bunny had bought the drug in question just last week."

"Bunny? Who's Bunny?"

"He said she's a cocktail waitress at the Empress. I'm going to check her out."

Tj stood up. "I'm coming with you. I've been here for over thirty minutes and I've drunk about as much coffee as I can. Besides, the barista behind the counter keeps glaring at me."

"Okay, but leave the talking to me."

"I get it. You're Batman, I'm Robin."

"Actually, I'm Batman and you're Alfred. I want you to hang back, maybe play a few slots, while I talk to the woman."

"I'm more of a blackjack girl. Slots are too passive for my taste."

"Whatever. Just stay out of the way. I wouldn't want you to get hurt."

"You think someone named Bunny can hurt me?"

"Tj..." Dylan warned.

"Okay, I'll play a few hands while you do the detective thing."

Walking into the casino was like entering a different world, one that was loud and bright and gaudy. "Looks like someone's having a good day," said Tj as they passed a woman jumping up and down and screaming at the top of her lungs as a river of quarters filled her tray. Most slot machines these days paid their winnings in the form of vouchers that could be cashed in at the nearest change booth, but Tj like the old-fashioned machines best, machines that provided tactile and auditory rewards as the coins clunk, clunk, clunked into the metal trays and had to be scooped into a cup.

Dylan parked Tj at a nearby slot machine before entering into a conversation with Bunny, who turned out to be a gorgeous blonde with silicone breasts. She initially swore she knew nothing about buying any drugs from Boots or anyone else. After Dylan dropped a few phrases like "twenty-four-hour lockup," the woman changed her tune and admitted she might have bought the drug after all for her boyfriend Troy, who had a client on the north shore.

"Troy?" Tj interrupted from the slot machine, where she had been doing more eavesdropping than gambling.

"Troy Potter."

"I know a Troy Potter," Tj said. "Graduated from Serenity

High a couple of years ago." Tj looked directly at Bunny. "You said he was your boyfriend? You do know he's married?"

The woman shrugged. "So? Most men want a little somethin' on the side, and as long as they have money I'm happy to oblige. I hope you aren't going to arrest Troy for dealin'. He's a good guy. Just needed to make a little extra money is all. He said a guy approached him who was willing to pay big bucks for the stuff."

"Do you know where Troy is now?" Dylan asked.

"At home, I guess."

"Did he say who the client was?" Tj asked.

Bunny shrugged. "Some old guy."

"Thank you for your time."

Tj was about to argue, but Dylan took her by the hand and led her away.

"Why did you let her go?" Tj asked. "You know those were the drugs used to kill Zachary."

"Bunny doesn't know who Troy sold the drugs to. I have an idea how we can find out."

CHAPTER 23

Saturday, October 30

The next morning Tj woke with a groan. A glance out her window confirmed that the sun had been up for hours. There was a note from Ashley on the table next to her bed: *Went to pumpkin patch with Kristi. Dennis said to let you sleep. Don't forget about the hayride and pumpkin lighting in the town square.* Dennis must have brought the girls home to grab a change of clothes at some point. Once she got Zachary's murder solved she was going to owe Dennis and Jenna big time for all the babysitting they were doing.

The hayride and annual jack-o'-lantern walk weren't until that evening. She was tempted to go back to sleep since she had most of a day all to herself for the first time in forever, but there was no way she was going to be able to relax until Zachary's murderer was behind bars.

Tj wandered into her bathroom and flipped on the countertop heater before turning the shower on high. Stripping off the thermals she'd worn to sleep, she stepped under the hot spray. Dylan was tracking down Troy, so the best use of her time would be to find out what the key she'd found in Zachary's box opened. She squeezed some of the rain-scented shampoo she'd bought at the boutique in town onto her head and rubbed it into a foamy cap that trailed down her back.

She'd thought a lot about the key, and the only thing she could come up with was that Zachary had opened a safety-deposit box at the bank. Of course, the fact that Zachary never left the house didn't bode well for the theory that he'd visited the local bank, but nothing else made sense.

Rinsing her hair, she applied a thick conditioner in a matching scent, then lathered her body with a moisturizing body wash, considering other options. He could have a lock box hidden somewhere in his house, a more feasible theory but much harder to prove or disprove. There might also be other lockers around town that could fit the key. In the movies, thieves often hid their ill-gotten gains in a bus or train station locker, but since Serenity had neither a bus nor a train station, she'd have to look elsewhere for her answer.

She rinsed her hair and body one final time, enjoying the powerful spray from the custom showerhead her dad had installed years earlier. Turning off the shower, she reached out for a thick, cream-colored towel and wrapped it around her petite frame. Wrapping a second towel around her hair, she stepped out onto the plush carpet and looked at her reflection in the mirror.

She supposed the best course of action was to try the bank. If the key didn't open a safety-deposit box, she'd return to Zachary's and look for a lock it might fit. Considering she'd had no idea about his safe, it actually made sense that he could have additional locked boxes or cabinets hidden around his mausoleum of a house.

After rubbing some the ridiculously expensive body lotion her grandpa had given her for Christmas onto her body, she dressed in a new pair of jeans and a white tank and dark blue V-neck sweater. Slipping a wide headband over the mass of shiny curls she'd partially dried, she applied a scant amount of makeup to her pale cheeks and a dash of mascara to the long lashes framing her bright blue eyes before heading down to the kitchen for a cup of coffee.

The house appeared to be empty. It was late as mornings at the resort went, and with the large number of guests staying with them this weekend, Tj imagined both her dad and grandfather were busy making sure everything was running smoothly. Taking her cup with her, she called Echo to her side and headed out the door to find her dad and fill him in on her plans. After that she figured she'd check on Shasta and her daughters and see how the baby calf, who seemed to be mending nicely, was doing with his new roommates.

An hour later, Tj walked through the festively decorated town as she made her way toward Serenity Community Bank. Tourists from as far away as the Bay Area visited Serenity on the last Saturday in October to participate in the largest pumpkin festival west of the Rocky Mountains. Thousands of jack-o'-lanterns had been carved for the annual event. Once the sun set and the sky grew dark, dozens of volunteers set out with butane lighters to bring the carved creations to life.

Turning the corner near the park where the gazebo was filled to capacity with pumpkins waiting for the carving contest later that afternoon, Tj smiled at the costumed children gathered in front of Hannigan's Toy Store, waiting patiently for the costume parade to begin. After waving at Frannie Edison crossing the crowded street, she made her way through the double doors of the bank. Proceeding directly to the customer service desk, Tj smiled at a middle-aged woman she recognized but whose name she couldn't remember.

"Can I help you?"

"I was wondering if you could tell me if this key belongs to one of your safety-deposit boxes."

The woman took the key and looked at it. "Yes, ma'am. Box seventy-two. Would you like to access it?"

"Yes, thank you." Tj couldn't believe it was going to be this easy.

"If you have ID, the key, and the code, I can show you to the back."

"Code?"

"The bank provides every box owner a key, but the code is provided by the lessee. No one else, not even the bank, has the code. I'm afraid without the code the key is quite useless."

"Terrific." Tj sighed.

"You forgot the code?" the woman asked.

"Actually, I'm not the one who opened the box. It belonged to my friend Zachary Collins. Mr. Collins passed away before he was able to give me the code. There must be some protocol for such occurrences."

The woman frowned. "Do you have your ID with you?"

Tj handed the woman her driver's license.

The woman compared the information on her screen to the license in her hand. "It appears the box was opened by a man named John Henry. He opened it on your behalf; the box is registered in your name. Unfortunately, the only way a box can be opened without the code is by court order. If Mr. Collins passed before providing you with the code, you can apply to the court for such an order, but I must warn you that making the request will most likely cause the box to be tied up in the probate process, which often takes a while."

Tj put her elbows on the counter and rested her head in her hands.

"If you knew Mr. Collins well, I suppose you could try to guess," the woman suggested. "The code has to be between five and ten numbers. Most people use something meaningful, such as a birthday, phone number, or social security number, if that helps."

"Can I try as many times as I want?" Tj asked.

"No. After five wrong tries the code is erased and it will take a court order to open the box."

Tj hesitated. She had no idea what the code was, but what did she really have to lose by trying? If she didn't succeed in five tries, she'd see if Dylan could get a court order to open the box. The customer service rep led her into the back room and pointed out the correct box. She showed Tj how to insert the key, then use the keypad to type in the code. She only had five tries, and the possibilities of combinations seemed endless.

Tj tried to think like Zachary would. The code for the puzzle box had been 8128. Only four numbers, and she needed at least five. She had no idea what his social security number was. She could try his birthday, but somehow she doubted he'd use that. Her birth date? Probably not. The answer to his puzzles had always been meaningful and obvious once figured out. Tj thought about their anniversary. She knew that day had meaning to Zachary. She tried it. Strike one.

Zachary had given her access to the box, so why hadn't he given her the code? The clue in the puzzle box had led to the safe. Maybe he wanted her to find the other items in the safe: the key and the phone number.

Tj typed in the seven-digit phone number: 438-9512. Strike two. Damn. Why else would he have the phone number of the bowling alley? Maybe the number wasn't a phone number after all. The marked keno numbers were 1, 2, 3, 4, 5, 6, 7, 8, 9. Nine numbers all in a row; the question was, should she enter them in order? She looked at the keno ticket. Zachary had circled the number fifteen even though it hadn't been marked to play. There had to be something significant about the number. Tj thought about how Zachary had used a perfect number to code the puzzle box. Chances were he was using the numbers from some other game he'd taught her.

Tj thought about all the possibilities. Zachary liked numbers. He'd taught her a lot of different ways to look at them. It made sense that the key to opening the box was something he'd shown her recently. Of course, Tj realized: the magic square puzzle they'd solved a few weeks earlier. Zachary had gone over it several times to make sure Tj understood how to build one. Tj quickly scratched a graph resembling a tic-tac-toe game on the back of the ticket. She remembered that to create a magic square you needed to have the numbers in each row as well as each column and each diagonal all add up to the same number. For a three-square puzzle the number each row needed to add up to was fifteen. Since there was more than one answer to the puzzle, Zachary would have left her an additional clue to make sure she came up with the specific order required.

Tj bit her lip as she tried to decide what that clue might be. She only had three tries left, so she couldn't just start punching in random sets. The phone number. She plugged the phone number into the graph:

438
951
2**.

That left six and seven. To create a magic square, you needed to put seven in the next box, followed by six. Tj wished she had more tries to see if her logic was correct, but the number sequence she had come up with seemed to be the best guess so she punched them in. She held her breath as the box popped open. Tj couldn't believe she had actually done it.

Slowly removing the box from the slot on the wall, she set it on the table and opened the top. Inside was a package wrapped in newspaper with her name on it. She wanted to wait and open it later, when she was alone and could really appreciate whatever it was Zachary had left her, so she slipped it into her bag. There were also two envelopes. The first envelope held a copy of the letter informing Maude and Millie that they'd won a contest, a copy of the letter offering a grant to Carmen, and a copy of the letter offering Kyle a job. Opening the second envelope, she gasped. She knew who the killer was.

Tj shoved everything into her bag and headed toward the sheriff's office.

"Do you think this will work?" Deputy Tim Matthews asked several hours later, sitting at a conference table with Dylan, Deputy Roy Fisher, and Tj.

"At this point it seems like our best bet," Roy answered.

"I think it's too dangerous," Dylan said.

"Tj can handle herself." There was a glint of merriment in Tim's eyes.

"I guess it's up to Tj." Roy turned to look directly at her. "What do you think? Can you do it?"

Were they kidding? She was numb trying to figure out what possessed her to think she wanted to play Nancy Drew. Even more than numb; she was terrified.

The plan, which she had to admit had been her idea in the first place, was the result of the second envelope she'd found which contained Zachary's will. A new will, that left the majority of his estate, including the house, to Kyle, as well as very generous bankrolls to Maude, Millie, and Carmen. The fact that Glen lied about the will and the house meant that he had to be the killer. The plan Tj came up with was to call Glen and arrange for him to meet her at the mansion on the pretext of providing him with important information. She was to lead him to the basement, which had limited access points, and pretend to open the safe in order to give him the coin collection Tj knew that he did not currently have access to. She was to engage him in conversation, getting him to admit to killing Zachary, and then Dylan would burst in through one door and Roy and Tim through the other.

"Tj?" Dylan tried to make eye contact. "Are you okay?"

She felt like she was in a coma. Maybe she was. The entire conversation would make more sense if she were dreaming.

"It's too much," she heard Dylan say. "We need to come up with something else."

"No." Tj finally spoke. "I can do this. I want to do this. I have to. For Zachary."

"Are you sure?" Tim asked. "We can come up with a different plan."

"I'm sure." Tj felt like she might throw up.

"Okay," Dylan said. "Call Glen and set up a meet for later this afternoon. That'll give us a chance to get everything into place. In the meantime, you should go home and get some rest."

Rest was the last thing she was going to be able to do, but there were some people she needed to talk to and now seemed as good a time as any.

CHAPTER 24

Once Tj got back to the resort she grabbed Echo and then headed over to the cabins. She'd finally begun to put together bits and pieces of conversations she'd had over the past week and a theory began to emerge. She figured that if her theory was correct, the news would affect Carmen the least, so she decided to start there. With Echo at her side, she knocked on Carmen's cabin door. What she hadn't counted on was Kyle's presence in her cabin.

"Tj, come in." Carmen, wearing gray sweatpants at least two sizes too big for her, answered the door. "And you too, Echo," she added as she opened the door wider to accommodate the dog's large frame.

When Echo saw that Kyle was also in attendance, he started to wag his tale and bounded across the small room to where Kyle sat on the floor beside the fire with Newton in his lap.

"Echo, down." Tj didn't want her overgrown dog to accidentally hurt the puppy in his enthusiasm to greet Kyle. Echo obediently laid down just inches from Kyle's outstretched hand. Kyle set Newton on the floor before turning to scratch the larger dog behind the ears.

"I'm glad you're here," Tj addressed Kyle. "I have something to tell you both. Let's let the dogs play while we talk at the table." She motioned toward the small dining table in the corner of the room.

The real log cabin was one of the resort's smaller units, with a living area featuring a river-rock fireplace on one wall and a kitchen nook on the other. Just off the living area was a moderate-size bedroom and a cozy bath with a shower but no tub. As with all the cabins at the Hideaway, behind the building was a private deck with a small hot tub that backed to the forest beyond.

"What's up?" Kyle asked after they were all seated.

"It's about your job," she looked at Kyle, "and your grant," she turned to Carmen.

"They're bogus, aren't they?" Carmen sounded disappointed.

"We'd begun to suspect as much when neither of us had heard anything," Kyle explained. "We compared letters and realized they were most likely written by the same person. I guess the job offer was too good to be true."

"Not necessarily," Tj said. "It's possible that both the job offer and the offer of a grant were legitimate. The man who wrote both letters was a good friend of mine, Zachary Collins."

"The man who died?" Carmen asked.

"Yeah, the man who died," Tj confirmed. "I found copies of both letters in his safety-deposit box. I believe that while there may very well be a real job and a real grant, my friend may have had ulterior reasons for bringing you here."

"Such as?" Kyle asked.

Tj stopped to think about what she was going to say. The way she presented the situation to the pair could make all the difference in how well they took the news. "It might be best to start at the beginning and sort of loop around to this point, if that's okay."

Kyle and Carmen looked at each other and seemed to exchange an unspoken agreement.

"My friend Zachary was a recluse during the fourteen years I knew him. He had extensive scars on his face which caused others to call him a monster. And while the face he lived with for most of his life was seriously disfigured, based on stories that others have told me, he was at one time a very rich and very handsome young man."

Tj took a breath before she continued. She had anticipated this conversation would be difficult for Kyle and Carmen but she hadn't anticipated how difficult it would be for her.

"Unfortunately Zachary's father was away much of the time and his mother had passed on early in his life, so although he was rich, he was also very lonely. He didn't work or attend college so he filled the hours of his life by partying, driving fast cars, and chasing beautiful women. Eventually, I'm not sure exactly when or how, he met a young woman who he fell madly in love with. The woman was married to another, and in fact had two young daughters, but she did not love her much older husband, so she decided to leave everything behind and run away with Zachary. During their time together Zachary and his young woman isolated themselves in his mansion so not a lot is known about their time together. What I do know is that the woman eventually became pregnant with Zachary's child."

Neither Kyle nor Carmen commented, although Tj could see the interest on their faces.

"Unfortunately the woman died in childbirth and the baby was given up for adoption. Zachary in his grief returned to his irresponsible ways and eventually was involved in a car accident in which he was driving and the man he was with was killed."

"This is a sad story, but what does it have to do with us?" Carmen asked.

"The man killed in the accident was named Timothy Bell. I remember you telling me that your Grandma Bell had eleven cats."

"Grandma Bell's husband was named Timothy. So you are saying that it was my grandfather that was killed in the accident which resulted in Zachary's scars?"

"Yes, I believe so. I believe that is why he brought you here."

"You think your friend brought me here to right this wrong by providing the funding for the study I'm working on?" Carmen clarified.

Tj nodded. She thought about telling her about the money Zachary had left her, which would easily fund multiple studies, but decided to wait until everyone was together.

Tj looked at Kyle who had yet to say anything. "The family who adopted Zachary's baby was named Donovan," Tj added.

"So what exactly are you saying?" Kyle asked. "That my dad was this man's son?"

"Yes, I believe he was. And I believe that the woman who birthed Zachary's son was Maude and Millie's mother, Mary."

"So Maude and Mille are really my half-aunts?"

"That's what I think. The story fits, and they have necklaces identical to one Zachary has. Zachary's Mary was wearing it in a photo he had. Maude mentioned that their mother died when they were babies, but I believe their father could have told them she was dead to cover her absence."

Tj held her breath while she allowed Kyle time to process everything. It was a lot to deal with.

Kyle smiled. "My mom is going to *love* them. From the first moment I met them, I kept thinking how well they'd fit in with our family. Now I guess I'll get the chance to see if I'm right. Do they know?"

"Not yet. I thought I'd head over there next."

"Maybe I should go with you." Kyle looked at Carmen. "Maybe we both should."

Deciding to leave Echo and Newton in Carmen's room, Tj, Kyle, and Carmen walked along the lakeshore path to Maude and Millie's cabin. Unlike Carmen's much simpler cabin, the cabin that had been reserved for Maude and Millie was one of their best.

"What a nice surprise." Maude answered the door. "Millie and I were just sharing a pot of coffee with the boys. Would you care for a cup?"

"No, thank you. We wondered if we might have a moment of your time."

"Certainly. Come on back to the deck. We have a fire going in the pit. It's actually quite warm if you cuddle up close to it."

"The thing we want to talk to you about is sort of personal." Tj glanced toward Abe and Andy.

"I'm sure whatever it is it will be fine to say in front of the boys," Maude responded.

There were four benches around the large fire pit. Each bench was long enough for two people of average size as long as they sat closely together. Andy and Maude were on one bench, Abe and Millie on another. Kyle and Carmen sat together, leaving Tj feeling like a third wheel—or seventh wheel, as the case may be.

"I'm not exactly sure how to approach this," Tj began. "I've thought about it quite a bit and have decided just to get right to the point."

"Of course, dear," Millie encouraged. "That's usually best."

"It's about the contest you won."

"Winning that contest was the luckiest thing that's happened to us in our whole lives." Maude smiled at Andy.

"I believe the letter you received actually came from a friend of mine, Zachary Collins." Tj studied everyone's faces to see if there was a glimmer of recognition.

"The man who had a necklace like ours?" Maude looked surprised. "Why would he pay for us to come here? We've never even met him."

"He knew your mother. At least I think he did. Was your mother's name Mary?"

"Well, yes, it was, but our mother has been dead for a long time."

"I realize your mother died, but I have reason to believe she didn't die when you thought she did. It seems my friend Zachary knew your mother after she left your father."

"Go on," Millie encouraged.

"I'm not sure what your father told you, but it seems your mother was married to your father at a very young age, probably no older than fifteen. She met Zachary, a handsome young man, when she was barely seventeen. I'm sure she loved you both very much, but from what I could find out, she fell in love with Zachary. She ran away with him and they lived—quite happily, I'm told—in his big old house on the lake."

Millie wiped a tear from her cheek.

"I'm sorry if this upsets you."

"I'm not upset. I'm glad our mama found some happiness in this life," Millie said.

"Besides," Maude added, "it explains a lot. Millie and I never could understand why the people in our congregation used to snicker when we'd speak of our dead mother and our poor, grieving father."

Tj was surprised at their reaction to the news. She'd

expected them to be...well, distraught that their mother had deserted them and their father had lied to them.

"Please understand," Millie added, "we loved our daddy. He guided us and took care of us. But Daddy was a hard, unbending man. We're not surprised our mother left him. We would have too had we the courage."

Tj couldn't quite reconcile in her mind the spunky twins she'd grown to know with women who would let themselves be subjugated all those years. She tried to imagine them full of life and curiosity yet waiting for sixty years until the death of the man who held them under his control set them free.

"So our mother lived a long life?" Maude asked.

"I'm afraid not. Shortly after she came to live with Zachary, she became pregnant and had a son. Unfortunately, she died as a result of a difficult labor."

"We have a brother?" Maude wondered.

Tj shook her head. "He died a few years ago. But he had a son, a man you recently met." She glanced over at Kyle.

Millie caught on. "We're your aunts?" She turned her full attention to the suddenly shy man.

"Appears so," Kyle said with a blush.

Both Maude and Mille began hugging and kissing him and asking a million questions. Tj thought about slipping out but still wanted to tell them about the will and the funeral that afternoon.

"I guess it's proof things come full circle," Millie said. "Zachary Collins may have taken away our mother, but by bringing us here he not only gave us the most precious gift of all—" she glanced at Abe "—but a new family as well. I'm sorry we never got to meet him."

Tj felt a tear threatening at the corner of her eye. "I think he would have enjoyed you too."

"Will there be a funeral?" Abe asked.

"Tomorrow. There's also a will."

By the time Tj had finished reading the will she felt completely drained. If she managed to get through the sting tonight and the funeral tomorrow, she'd probably sleep for a week.

CHAPTER 25

Tj drove through the streets of Serenity as the sun dipped behind the mountain. She knew Dylan and the others were already positioned at Zachary's estate. Waiting, watching, ready to respond at a moment's notice. Tj could hear her heart pounding as she pulled up to the front gate. She wondered if the others could hear it through the wire she was wearing.

Opening the tall, wrought-iron gate, she drove slowly down the private road before pulling into the circular drive in front of the house. She turned off the engine and looked at the dark structure. For a moment she remembered happier visits: the first time she snuck onto the estate in answer to a dare from her friends; the terror she'd felt when she first saw Zachary staring out a window as she tried to sneak silently onto the front porch; her laughter when Zachary smiled at her and she knew he wasn't the monster everyone thought.

An empty car was in the drive. He must already be waiting inside. She wondered how he'd gotten in, then realized it really didn't matter. All that mattered was getting through the next few minutes alive. She took a deep breath and tried to calm her nerves. Her hand was shaking so badly, she could barely unbuckle her seat belt, but somehow she found a way.

Tj picked up her jacket and slipped it on as she stepped out of the car. It wasn't cold, but she found she couldn't stop shivering. She paused after slowly making her way up the front steps. *Just breathe.* She turned the knob and opened the door. The man who'd murdered one of her best friends was sitting in the same chair in which she'd found Zachary's dead body. Tj had to bite the inside of her lip to keep from blurting out how truly morbid that was.

"You wanted to talk?" Glen asked.

Tj paused and tried to act nonchalant, as if she had all the time and not a care in the world. She knew that in negotiations such as this it was the person with the least investment in the outcome who maintained the upper hand.

"I stumbled onto something I thought you might be interested in," Tj began.

"Yes?"

Tj walked across the room before answering. She closed the drape on the front window before sitting down on the sofa. "As you know, Zachary and I were good friends. He told me everything, things he didn't tell anyone else." Tj paused, letting the suspense build.

"Such as?"

Tj leaned forward, placing her elbows on her knees. "The location of a coin collection worth over a million dollars, to start." Tj discovered that the gift Zachary had left for her in the safety deposit box was the very coin collection they were using for bait.

"Coin collection?"

"I'm sure Zachary must have mentioned it." Tj sat back, crossing her arms in front of her as if bored with the entire conversation.

"I know his father had such a collection, but Zachary never mentioned it. I figured it was sold off years ago."

"No, he still had it."

"Why are you telling me this?"

"I want a cut. I realize I could just take the coins but there is one coin specifically that is very rare and is worth almost a quarter of the value of the collection. The coin has been authenticated and is insured. The problem is that if I try to sell it any legit buyer will want authentication that I actually own the coin. I could lie or try to sell it on the black market but it's a risk and I have sisters to think of. I figured since you are in charge of liquidating the estate you could legally sell the collection and give me half."

"It seems fishy that you'd want to steal from Zachary's estate. I know you were friends."

"Exactly! I was Zachary's *best* friend. His only friend. After years of giving up hours upon hours of my time to visit with him and see to his wellbeing, he left me nothing. Not a single token of his appreciation." It actually caused Tj physical pain to say this but she knew she needed to give Glen a reason to trust her, or at least believe her. "After everything I did for the man I figure I'm due this."

"You have the coins with you?" Glen finally asked.

"They're in the safe."

"You have the combination?"

"I do."

"What do you say we take a look?"

"Okay." Tj willed herself to stay calm. "Safe's in the basement."

Tj led him though the house, down the stairs, and into the basement. She closed the basement door behind them so Dylan could get into place without being noticed. Her heart was pounding so hard, she feared it might burst through her chest. She slowly made her way across the room, then removed the picture of the Model T, revealing the existence of the safe.

"Pretty smart the way you set up Zachary's murder to look like a suicide." Tj slowly turned the dial to the left.

The man shrugged but didn't say anything.

Tj turned the dial to the right. She knew they'd need more.

"It was genius, really. No defensive wounds or signs of foul play to tip off the cops."

"How about a little less talking and a little more dialing?" Glen was obviously trying to hurry her along.

Tj purposely passed the third number before trying to open the safe. "Guess I missed a number."

"You playing me?" He pulled a small gun from his pocket and pointed it at her head.

Tj tried to look unaffected. She knew from watching the detective shows she loved so much that it was best in situations like this to maintain a sense of calm and control. "I'm just nervous. I'll try again."

"Best make sure there are no more mistakes."

Tj turned back toward the safe and started the dialing sequence over. "I have to admire your guts," Tj tried again. "Not many men with balls enough to kill a man."

The man remained stubbornly silent. Dylan said they needed a confession.

"Was it you who drank the scotch?"

"Yeah, so? Old man was never going to drink it. Seemed like a waste."

Tj stopped dialing and turned around. "Why'd you kill him? Zachary was an old man who didn't have long left anyway. Why not just wait for him to die a natural death?"

"You have ten seconds to get that safe open or I pull the trigger and put a bullet in your pretty little head."

"Just curious." Tj turned back toward the safe. "I just

figured a strong, intelligent man like you would have enough discipline to wait."

"He was going to give the money away."

"So you drugged him?"

"What choice did I have? He planned to make some big announcement about the new will at the ball this weekend. He said he was going to make amends to the people he'd hurt the most."

"Did he suffer?" Tj couldn't help but ask.

"Why are you asking so many questions?" Glen grabbed her arm and turned her to face him, pointing the gun directly at her forehead. "You best get that safe open before I lose my patience."

"Already lost mine." Tj kneed Glen in the groin with every bit of strength her hundred-pound body could muster. Luckily, with twenty-two years of martial arts training, a hundred pounds of force was enough. Glen groaned as he bent over, gasping for air. Tj kicked the gun from his hand as Dylan burst in through one door, Roy and Tim through the other.

"Did you get enough?"

"We got enough." Dylan held up a tape recorder. "By the way, sounded like a nice move with the gun. Where'd you learn to do that?"

Tj shrugged. The fact that she was a fighter as a kid, prompting her dad to sign her up for martial arts classes in the hope she would learn discipline, was common knowledge. The fact she'd stuck with them ever since was a story for another day.

By the time Tj got home it was almost seven o'clock, she was drained, and she hadn't eaten a thing all day. She felt herself dragging as she returned to the house. All she wanted was a sandwich, a hot bath, and her cozy bed. It had been a long, emotional week and tomorrow promised to be a long, emotional day.

"Good, you're here," Ashley greeted her the minute she walked in the door. "I told Kristi we'd meet them downtown for the jack-o'-lantern stroll by seven thirty at the latest. If we don't leave right this minute, we'll never make it."

The Pumpkin Festival. She had totally forgotten about the Pumpkin Festival.

"You forgot," Ashley accused.

"I did not," Tj lied. "Gracie ready?" She put her hand on her growling stomach.

"She's waiting in the other room."

"Okay, just let me grab an apple to eat on the way."

CHAPTER 26

Sunday, October 31

The small cemetery, on land Jeremiah Collins had donated to the town, was at the end of a narrow road on the northernmost corner of the estate. A tall rock wall separated it from the now public land. Tj shivered as the cold wind whistled through the treetops. There was something unnerving about standing on ground where multiple generations of the families she knew and loved were buried. The Collins family had kept a corner of the public cemetery private. The fenced-off section was large enough for several generations of large families, but in the past hundred years only seven people had been buried there. The location Zachary had picked out for his own final resting place was surrounded by towering pines and colorful aspens.

The group gathered around Zachary Collins's final resting place was larger than Tj would ever have imagined. Pastor Dan stood alone behind the closed casket, while Tj and Kyle stood directly across from him, holding hands as they said their final good-byes. Although Tj had just met Kyle a few days before, she felt a special affection for him.

Slightly behind them and to Kyle's left stood Carmen,

Maude, Mille, Abe, and Andy, an odd group that had been brought together by Zachary's final bequest. In life Zachary had touched the lives of few, but with his death new relationships had been born, relationships, Tj suspected, that would continue long after Zachary's "family" had returned to their homes.

To Tj's right and slightly behind the group Zachary had assembled stood Jenna, with her husband Dennis and mother Helen. Tj's dad stood with Rosalie, Frannie Edison, Hazel Whipple, Prudence Holland, Jeff Warren, and Nick and Emma Grainger, as well as her Grandpa Ben and his friends, Bookman and Doc. Tj smiled as she remembered the look of both shock and pleasure on Kyle's face when she'd introduced him to Bookman. A part of the family for the past fifteen years, Tj often forgot that for much of the world he was a widely read and much loved author.

Tj felt a tear slip down her cheek as Dan began to speak. Her relationship with Zachary had been an odd one by anyone's definition, but she was a better person for having had him in her life. She'd miss the chess games, the puzzle boxes he'd built for her, and the riddles he'd spent hours coming up with. She'd miss the look of delight in his eye as she walked through the door and his look of childlike anticipation as she tried to solve one of his puzzles.

Dan began, "We are gathered here together to say a final good-bye to a man few of us actually knew. Mr. Collins sent me a letter a few weeks ago, specifying his burial instructions and asking me to read his final words to anyone who might attend this farewell."

Dan unfolded a piece of paper and began to read: "As I approach the end of my time on this earth, I find that I am filled with remorse for deeds left undone. The lives I could have touched but chose not to. The people I could have helped if I'd allowed myself to live in the world rather than in isolation. The love and joy I could have shared if I'd allowed others to penetrate my sturdy wall of self-loathing. I've lived a selfish life, a solitary life, a life served in penance, and my passing will affect no one. There has, however, been one bright spot in my otherwise empty world. Without that light I would not have found the courage to embark on the journey to which I have committed my life these past few months. A journey that I hope will serve to rectify in some small way the pain and suffering I have caused to others.

"As I write this, I have a plan to bring the people I have hurt the most to my little corner of the world, to beg for their forgiveness and to offer them each a small gift as atonement for my sins. If I have been successful and they have accepted my meager offering, they may be here to witness these final words. If not, then the words should still be spoken, for there is nothing sadder than words left unsaid.

"Maude and Millie, words cannot express the depth of my sorrow for taking, not only from your young lives, but also from an otherwise dark world, the light of your mother's smile. She was a beautiful woman, a caring woman, a woman full of laughter and sunshine. I loved her from the moment I laid eyes on her. Her very presence brought meaning and purpose to my empty soul. But in the end my selfish need to possess her destroyed her. I have no right to ask for your forgiveness since I cannot forgive myself, but I want you to know that your mother loved you very much.

"Carmen, I've spent many hours trying unsuccessfully to come up with words to express my remorse for the part I played in the death of your grandfather. I don't know why I lived and he died. I've served my life in penance for this unforgivable act, but as my own time draws to an end, I've realized that if I had a hundred more years to suffer for my sins, it still would not be long enough to atone for what I have done.

"And Kyle, I cannot begin to express to you the joy I felt when I found that I had a grandson. I have only a short time left on this earth, but every one of those days will be filled with the agony of conflicted emotions as I mourn the loss of the son I never knew and rejoice in the gift of the grandson I still hope to meet. I couldn't love your father. I was young and foolish and blamed him for your mother's death. I realize now that had I chosen love over abandonment, the very existence of this miracle conceived in love would have changed the course of my life forever.

"And, finally, Tj. I am unsure if the others are here. I am, however, confident that my eulogy has been heard by at least one set of ears. I cannot begin to express to you how much you have meant to me in these final years. I'd lived a life of self-imposed darkness for so long that when you came to my door on that Halloween night, fearless in your quest to impress your young friends, and smiled a greeting to this worthless old man, I knew in an instant my life would be forever changed. God had sent me an angel to guide me on the final leg of my life's journey. A beacon in the darkness, you reminded me what it was to be alive, to laugh and feel long-forgotten emotions such as love and joyful anticipation. I wish I could have taken your gift of life and allowed it to make a real change in my life. I wish I could have found the courage to leave my prison and share my life with others. I'm afraid I am neither as fearless nor as kindhearted as you, my young friend. But I want you to know that of all the lives you've rescued and all the strays you've adopted, there is no other lonely soul more grateful than mine."

By the time Dan had finished reading and begun the familiar passage that begins with "Ashes to ashes," there wasn't a dry eye in the cemetery. Tj and Kyle hugged each other and cried for the man who had touched their lives in vastly different ways. Tj had known the man, had shared his life and, in doing so, had given him the courage to reach out to others. Kyle had never known the man, but with his money he now had the opportunity to touch lives and do the good deeds to which Zachary could never bring himself.

"Beautiful service." Dylan approached Tj as the mourners headed to their cars.

"Where'd you come from?" she asked, surprised at his sudden appearance.

"I was watching from the back. I didn't want to intrude on the mourning of those who knew the man, but I wanted to stop by and offer my condolences."

Tj turned and looked at what was left of the crowd. "The truth of the matter is, most of the people here never met Zachary. They were just folks going about their lives who got pulled into his story in one way or another over the past week. It's sad their paths never crossed when he was alive. I think he would have really enjoyed knowing them." Tj turned and looked at Dylan. "Are you going to the ball tonight?"

"Wasn't going to. You?"

"Yeah. I actually wish I could just go home and relax but I promised Helen, and a promise is a promise."

CHAPTER 27

Halloween night

The Black and Black Ball was held each year at the historic Timberlake House. Built in 1922, the house had once been the summer mansion of shipping heir Jason Timberlake. During the mid-1970s the Timberlake family had donated the house, along with ten acres of land and several smaller cabins and outbuildings, to the town of Serenity. The town established the Timberlake Historical Society which rented the facility for weddings and other special events.

Most years Tj put together the goriest costume she could think of, but this year she had promised to let Helen dress her, a decision she regretted after what seemed like an eternity of plucking and preening, curling and polishing. Helen had chosen an extremely heavy gown in a gorgeous sapphire blue featuring a full bell-shaped skirt, tight bodice, and puff sleeves. The dress was meant to be worn with undergarments designed to bind and reshape, but Tj took one look at the torture devices worn by her ancestors and decided to let her ample bosom spill where it may. After having her nails painted, her brows shaped, and her hair washed, she poured herself into the form-fitting dress, then sat perfectly still as Helen arranged her long hair into ringlets befitting a nineteenth-century woman. Tj vowed to never again subject herself to such a grueling experience.

Then she looked in the mirror. She looked different. Not just different but stunning. The dress, which perfectly matched her eyes, accentuated her petite but curvy figure. The diamond earrings, which had been her grandmother's, reflected the light as she twirled in a circle. Her hair, sleek and controlled, looked the best it ever had and probably ever would. When she arrived at the ball everyone in the room turned to look at her, and for the first time in her life, Tj felt like a princess.

It was the most magical night of her life. For about twenty minutes. And then the weight of the dress, the pinching of her undergarments, and the perfectly applied but untouchable makeup, left her longing for her comfy sweats and the cozy sofa waiting for her at home. Maybe being a princess wasn't all it was cut out to be.

Tj headed over to the table where Kyle, who was dressed as a vampire, and Carmen, who was a scientist, were sitting.

"Let me guess." Tj smiled at Carmen as she sat down beside her. "This is pretty much how you dress every day." She gestured to the white lab coat.

"Hey, I'm a starving student. I couldn't afford to spend money on a costume I was going to wear only once. Maybe next year I'll go as something exotic."

"You think you'll be back next year?"

"Well…" Carmen glanced at Kyle. "Next year is a long way off. I'll have to see how things go, but I'll definitely be back for the wedding."

"Wedding?"

"My new aunts," Kyle explained. "They told us earlier they're going to be married during the Winter Carnival. I guess you made it sound like the ideal honeymoon. They've already booked their rooms."

"Really? That was quick."

"Millie said at their age time was their most precious commodity and they didn't want to wait."

"How about you?" Tj asked Kyle. "Any big plans for your newfound money?"

"Honestly, it's a lot to process. I know I don't want to sell the house to that developer. That new deputy got Keller to admit the sales agreement he offered Mr. Benson was a fake and therefore not binding. Since I find myself between jobs, I thought maybe I'd fix up the place. I need to go home for a few weeks to get Trooper and the rest of my stuff, but I should be back by mid-November."

"That's really awesome. When you get ready to start the remodel I can point you in the direction of some excellent contractors."

"Thanks. I'd appreciate that."

Tj glanced toward the front of the room where Jenna and Dennis, who had just arrived, were talking with a friend. "I'm going to go and say hi to Jenna. You guys have a wonderful evening."

Tj made her way across the room to where her best friend was standing. "You're late."

"Dennis got off early, so after your grandpa picked up the girls for trick-or-treating, we decided to open a bottle of champagne and one thing led to another." Jenna blushed.

Tj grinned as Jenna leaned into Dennis, who had put his arm around her.

"So, has anyone told you how stunning you look?" Dennis complimented.

"Yeah, you really do," Jenna added.

"I know. It's amazing what results you can get with hours upon hours of being plucked and polished. Of course, it took a whole team and most of the afternoon to get this result, so I'm thinking I'd better track down someone to take a picture because I can promise you I'll never subject myself to such torture again. I have no idea how women had time to do anything else when this was the style."

"I don't think they did much else," Jenna pointed out. "Being beautiful was sort of their job. Land a rich husband and your life was considered a success."

"I think I prefer a life where I'm more than just someone's wife." Tj tried to adjust the bra that was being pinched by the tight bodice. "And I really prefer being able to breath. This dress is so heavy I feel like I'm walking around in a body cast. How about you, Dennis? Ever wish you had a trophy wife?"

"No way. Personally, I like a woman I can touch without fear of messing up her hair or getting stabbed by her corset." Dennis kissed his wife. "I love having a wife with whom I can raise a family, and go bowling with, and go to the bar and eat chicken wings with."

Dennis looked deeply into Jenna's eyes. Running his finger along her cheek, he tucked her long blond hair behind one ear before kissing her slowly and ever so softly on the lips. "Wanna dance?"

Jenna hesitated and looked at her friend, who would be left standing alone.

"Go ahead," Tj said. "I think I'll go and say hi to Maude and Millie." Tj smiled as she watched the couple sway to the music. Secretly Tj was jealous of Jenna. Not because Dennis was firm and fit and gorgeous from hours upon hours of training, but because Dennis was goofy and romantic and loved his wife with every fiber of his being. For the most part Tj was happy with her life, but someday she wanted what they had, the stuff of fairy tales.

Tj watched her friends for a while longer and then headed across the room to join Maude and Millie, who were dressed like cowgirls, and Abe and Andy, who were dressed like farmers. They were sitting at a table near the dance floor sipping champagne and watching those who were dancing.

"Tj, how are you dear?" Millie hugged her when she approached. "Did you hear the news?"

"I did. Congratulations."

"We feel like we're walking on sunshine," Maude gushed. "If we'd have known what we were missing, we would have defied Daddy and left the group years ago."

"But then you might not have met Abe and Andy," Tj pointed out.

"How right you are, dear." Mille leaned her head against Abe's arm. "I've been waiting my whole life for this, and I plan to make the most of every minute."

"Your costume is lovely," Millie added. "You look just like a fairy princess. Perhaps Sister and I should wear dresses like that for our wedding. Antique dresses for antique brides."

"You're hardly an antique," Tj said. "Besides these old dresses are made with heavy material and weigh a ton."

"Perhaps you're right. Sister and I have always dreamed of making a dramatic entrance down an elegant staircase. I guess it'd be better to wear something we can walk in comfortably."

"Where are you planning to have the ceremony?"

"Here, actually," Maude said. "We were lucky to get it on such short notice. Apparently someone canceled just minutes before we called to inquire about it. Now if that isn't fate, I don't know what is."

Tj could picture the delightful sisters in their wedding

finery. She was happy that after years of living in isolation they'd found a second chance at life. After talking to the sisters a while longer, Tj wandered over to chat with her dad, who was having a drink at the bar with Hank Hammond, the winner of this year's chili cook-off.

"How's my princess?" Mike turned on his bar stool to kiss Tj on the cheek as she walked over to stand behind him.

"Suffocating." Tj tried to take a deep breath, but the tight bodice prevented her from doing so. "You look very handsome in your police officer costume. Where's your biker chick?"

"Rosalie is making the rounds. Hank and I decided to sit it out and have a cold one instead."

"Mind if I join you? These shoes are killing me."

"Where's your prince?" Hank pulled out a bar stool so she could sit down.

"Darn, I knew I forgot something. Did the girls get back from trick-or-treating before you left?" Tj asked her dad. Her grandpa had taken Ashley, Gracie, Kristi, and Kari trick-or-treating so Helen could work her magic on Tj.

"Yeah. They seemed to have had a good time. Kristi and Kari are spending the night. Grandpa was getting them settled in front of the television in the den and Helen was making popcorn when I left."

"Curling up on the sofa in front of the television eating a bowl of popcorn sounds wonderful. I don't think I'm cut out for this princess thing. Unlike Cinderella, I have serious doubts as to whether I'll make it to midnight. I think I'll just call a cab and go home."

"I'll give you a ride. Rosalie seemed like she was tired and thinking of an early night."

"Okay, thanks, Dad."

Tj was on her way to tell Jenna she was going to leave early when Dylan walked in. Dressed not in a costume but in his deputy sheriff uniform, he still managed to cause Tj's heart to skip a beat.

"You came." She smiled.

"Couldn't miss out on a dance with the prettiest girl in town. Have you seen her?" he teased.

"Very funny." Tj punched him in the arm.

Dylan playfully rubbed his arm. "Got quite a punch for a little thing. By the way, you look beautiful."

"Take a good look," Tj twirled in a circle, "because this Cinderella is about to go home and turn back into a much more comfortable homely stepsister."

"Don't tell anyone," Dylan said, leaning in close and whispering, "but I've always had a thing for homely stepsisters."

"Really?" Tj smiled.

"Really. Much less pretentious. In fact, if you really are ready to go, maybe after you unrig yourself we can stop by the hotel. I can change and then we can get a bite. I've had the strangest craving for chicken wings all day."

"Seriously? Chicken wings?"

"I guess I should buy you something more befitting a princess. Maybe a steak?"

"Chicken wings sound perfect." Tj looped her arm through Dylan's. "Come on. I need to tell my dad that I'm leaving and then we're out of here. And since we're on the subject of personal preferences, how do you feel about bowling?"

KATHI DALEY

Kathi Daley lives with her husband, kids, grandkids, and Bernese mountain dogs in beautiful Lake Tahoe. When she isn't writing, she likes to read (preferably at the beach or by the fire), cook (preferably something with chocolate or cheese), and garden (planting and planning, not weeding). She also enjoys spending time in the water, hiking, biking, and snowshoeing. Kathi uses the mountain setting in which she lives, along with the animals (wild and domestic) that share her home, as inspiration for her five cozy mystery series: Zoe Donovan, Whales and Tails Island, Tj Jensen, Sand and Sea Hawaiian, and Seacliff High Teen.

The Tj Jensen Mystery Series
by Kathi Daley

PUMPKINS IN PARADISE (#1)

SNOWMEN IN PARADISE (#2)

BIKINIS IN PARADISE (#3)

CHRISTMAS IN PARADISE (#4)

PUPPIES IN PARADISE (#5)

HALLOWEEN IN PARADISE (#6)

TREASURE IN PARADISE (#7)

Henery Press Mystery Books

And finally, before you go...
Here are a few other mysteries
you might enjoy:

PRACTICAL SINS
FOR COLD CLIMATES

Shelley Costa

A Val Cameron Mystery (#1)

When Val Cameron, a Senior Editor with a New York publishing company, is sent to the Canadian Northwoods to sign a reclusive bestselling author to a contract, she soon discovers she is definitely out of her element. Val is convinced she can persuade the author of that blockbuster, The Nebula Covenant, to sign with her, but first she has to find him.

Aided by a float plane pilot whose wife was murdered two years ago in a case gone cold, Val's hunt for the recluse takes on new meaning: can she clear him of suspicion in that murder before she links her own professional fortunes to the publication of his new book?

When she finds herself thrown into a wilderness lake community where livelihoods collide, Val wonders whether the prospect of running into a bear might be the least of her problems.

Available at booksellers nationwide and online

Visit www.henerypress.com for details

TELL ME NO LIES

Lynn Chandler Willis

An Ava Logan Mystery (#1)

Ava Logan, single mother and small business owner, lives deep in the heart of the Appalachian Mountains, where poverty and pride reign. As publisher of the town newspaper, she's busy balancing election season stories and a rash of ginseng thieves.

And then the story gets personal. After her friend is murdered, Ava digs for the truth all the while juggling her two teenage children, her friend's orphaned toddler, and her own muddied past. Faced with threats against those closest to her, Ava must find the killer before she, or someone she loves, ends up dead.

Available at booksellers nationwide and online

Visit www.henerypress.com for details

MURDER ON A SILVER PLATTER

Shawn Reilly Simmons

A Red Carpet Catering Mystery (#1)

Penelope Sutherland and her Red Carpet Catering company just got their big break as the on-set caterer for an upcoming blockbuster. But when she discovers a dead body outside her house, Penelope finds herself in hot water. Things start to boil over when serious accidents threaten the lives of the cast and crew. And when the film's star, who happens to be Penelope's best friend, is poisoned, the entire production is nearly shut down.

Threats and accusations send Penelope out of the frying pan and into the fire as she struggles to keep her company afloat. Before Penelope can dish up dessert, she must find the killer or she'll be the one served up on a silver platter.

Available at booksellers nationwide and online

Visit www.henerypress.com for details

Made in the USA
San Bernardino, CA
24 November 2019

60371472R00131